Be ɪʋɪce

Anabel Donald has been writing fiction since 1982 when her first novel, *Hannah at Thirty-five*, was published to great critical acclaim. In her thirty-six-year teaching career she has taught adolescent girls in private boarding schools, a comprehensive and an American university. Most recently, she has written the five Alex Tanner crime novels in the *Notting Hill* series.

BE NICE

ANABEL DONALD

JONATHAN CAPE
LONDON

Published by Jonathan Cape 2002

2 4 6 8 10 9 7 5 3 1

First published in Great Britain in 2002 by Jonathan Cape
Random House, 20 Vauxhall Bridge Road,
London SW1V 2SA

Random House Australia (Pty) Limited
20 Alfred Street, Milsons Point, Sydney,
New South Wales 2061, Australia

Random House New Zealand Limited
18 Poland Road, Glenfield,
Auckland 10, New Zealand

Random House (Pty) Limited
Endulini, 5A Jubilee Road, Parktown 2193, South Africa

The Random House Group Limited Reg. No. 954009

A CIP catalogue record for this book is available
from the British Library

ISBN 0-224-06308-1

Papers used by The Random House Group Limited are natural,
recyclable products made from wood grown in sustainable forests;
the manufacturing processes conform to the environmental
regulations of the country of origin

Typeset by Palimpsest Book Production Limited,
Polmont, Stirlingshire
Printed and bound in Great Britain by
Mackays of Chatham plc, Chatham, Kent

Dedication to come

CHAPTER ONE

Wonderful winner: Alice, 18
From: Bishop's Stortford, UK
Hair: auburn
Eyes: brown
Sibs: none
Fave celebs: Madonna
Princess Diana
Wrote about: co-operation
Cares about: world poverty
Uses: too right! (lubricated tampon for medium to heavy flow)

I always wake straight up: deep asleep, blink, completely awake, blink, blink. It's one of the many great things about being me. My eyes snap right open, I don't look blurred, but sharp, and I think sharp too. This morning: Crash! Survived! Yes!

I stretched gracefully, like a cat, and checked out the bod. Gooood. Nearly as perfect as ever, bit of bruising. Bare feet: must've lost the shoes, never mind, crap shoes anyway, competition shoes like everyone else's. After the crash, Dads'll be wetting himself,

I

missing me. It'll rain shoes. I'll need another cupboard to put all the gear he'll buy me.

No comb either, that's worse. Gotta get the hair in shape to meet the rescuers, meet the cameras. Flash flash, maybe not flash because they'll come in the daytime, click click, this way, Alice, look over here, Alice, and I'll hold my face just right like Mums taught me, useful she was a model, she doesn't know much about much but she knows about presentation, and Dads says in the twenty-first century presentation's 110% of everything. So I'll fix the smile then keep refreshing it so it doesn't look fixed, and by then I'll have a comb.

Toes still look good. Green and silver. I've great feet. Strong. Shapely. Something crawling on them, yuk. Insects. Hop hop shake feet, bye bye insects. Must pee. Mustn't squat down too far when I pee. First I pee, then I go find people.

Wonderful winner: Anneka, 11
From: Doncaster, UK
Hair: brown
Eyes: blue
Sibs: none
Fave celebs: Sean Connery
Wrote about: Bullies
Cares about: getting it right
Uses: right starter! (slimline towel: recommended for beginners)

I sleep even when I'm scared. Acksherly I sleep more when I'm scared, and the crash was scary. I was sure

I was going to die. Then the banging and the huge noise stopped and I hadn't died, I could move. At the plane door, we all sort of wedged. I could of got through easily on my own but not with the big girl I was pulling with me, so I stamped and kicked and elbowed and everyone squealed and we all popped out, splosh into the water. Then in the water the great wind was blowing, too much to stand up, and the big girl just, like, froze. It was OK in the water but she was really big and heavy to push and pull on land. I did get her across the beach and into a hollow thing just behind the beach, a bit out of the wind. Then I went to sleep.

The storm stopped when it still wasn't proply light. You could see a bit. I checked my body, it was OK. Sore bits which'd be bruises soon, and grazes on my knees n elbows with great scab potential. I like picking scabs even better than picking my nose. Only when I'm alone, otherwise it'd be gross. Acksherly I felt fine, sort of zingy, which was weird cos people'd died, lots of them.

My big girl hadn't died, though. She was breathing. Asleep probly but could be in a coma, big bruise on her forehead. I sort of tried to wake her, but she grunted and turned over so I left her, to be useful before she woke up. Earn your keep, be useful, Granpa says. We needed water and food, so I went to find it.

I went to the beach to see if anyone else was about yet. They weren't. The back half of the plane, the bit we'd been in, was still stuck on the reef. I could of gone in to see if anyone was alive in there, but I didn't.

3

My reasons for this were 1) it was still quite dark 2) I'm not tall or strong so I couldn't do much for them 3) I'm a coward.

Granpa says, know your limitations, so I don't feel too bad about being a coward, just a bit.

Anyway if I couldn't be brave I could be useful so I took the biggest shell I could find, washed the sand off it in the sea (the sea was warm) and went into the trees, where I could hear running water.

Alice, 18, 5'8", mid-brown hair with red highlights: It was well out of order that nobody'd come to find me. Let alone how out of order it was that the sodding plane crashed. Hey! Hey, guys, over here! I shouted, standing on the beach at the point near where I'd come out of the trees, because catch me walking anywhere I don't have to. The Pilates and the gym bike's enough, thanks very much.

Kids started popping out of the bushes, mostly one by one, all in the competition kit, same as me, chinos and the bright yellow sweatshirt with *right!* on the front. Lucky I look great in yellow.

What's happened to the real people? Bloody hell! They can't *all* have died, it doesn't make sense. Don't tell me, it's just these *kids*. Sod it. A load of whiny kids, all above themselves because they won the competition.

Still, make no enemies till you're sure they're losers. Hi, guys, I said.

Anneka, 11, 5'1", mousy hair: When I got back with a shell-full of water (carry carefully, both hands,

4

don't spill) the big girl kept sleeping even though I nudged her. I thought she was putting it on. Girls her age put everything on and it gets up my nose because I like things straight. Granpa doesn't like females much. He says when they grow tits, they go mad. He says it quite often. All the time, acksherly. Sometimes I believe it and it worries me, what'll happen to me when I grow tits, which I absolutely haven't yet.

Anyway it was past time the big girl woke up and drank my water. The sun was proply rising. She needed to see it cos it was amazing, the sky all bright bright yellow shading into green and colours popping up everywhere out of the grey.

'I know you're awake,' I said in her ear. It could of been I said it VERY loudly, I sometimes do.

The girl groaned. I felt really guilty. Maybe she wasn't pretending. The bruise on her head was HUGE now. It couldn't of grown in the time, must of just looked like it, cos I was sorry for shouting. It was a horrible reddy-black bump, anyhow. And last night after the crash, she'd been totally out of it, moaning and thrashing around. She'd of stayed in her seat if I hadn't pulled her out, and then kind of steered her around. She didn't talk to me even after I'd got her to the hollow and put her in the recovery position and checked her airway was clear like I'd learnt in first aid. I'd probly saved her life, acksherly, and I didn't want her dying now. I sort of sploshed water into her mouth with my fingers, cos you always need water, it stands to reason.

AGES passed. I'd had another wee, I'd topped up the water, and I'd picked my second-best scab till it bled. It was well time the big girl kept me company, coma or not. Sides, she was just pretending to be asleep. And I was scared. There were people on the beach, walking about, and they were all girls.

I started shaking her, seriously hard, and shouting, 'WAKE UP!'

Wonderful winner: Emma, 17
From: Oxford, UK
Hair: blonde
Eyes: blue
Sibs: elder sister Christie, 19
Fave celebs: Octavia Hill
Wrote about: making a
contribution
Cares about: the one she's with
Uses: too right! (lubricated tampon for medium to heavy flow)

OK, OK, I'll get up. The voice was right, of course, I'd been semi-awake for ages, but my head hurt like stink and while I burrowed into the leaves I could pretend it was the duvet at home, and that the only part of my body I could feel was the bit round my mouth which was still tingling nicely from saying goodbye to Rick.

'Wake up, please wake up.' She was squeaking by now, sounding panic-stricken, poor kid. 'Wake up. Please. Drink this. Here. It's fresh water. I washed the shell in fresh water too so it'll be all right. I got it from a rainwater pool.'

I sat up, drank the water, looked at her. She'd sat

next to me in the plane. I'd already had hours and hours of the flight to notice that she was skinny, with short mousy hair and a motormouth.

'Remember, I was next to you in the plane. I ate your cake, the cake you didn't want with your lunch after Honolulu, you gave it to me. We're on an island. There's lots of us winners got out, but no grown-ups I can see. Most of them're down there. Look.' She pointed. 'I tried to count but they keep moving about. I got to twenty-something but I might've counted some of them twice. You all right? There's blood on your head but it's dry. You all right?'

'I'm OK,' I said to reassure her, though actually my head felt as if an axe was sticking in it, above my right ear.

'Because I think we should go to the plane and see if anyone needs help, the back bit of the plane I mean because it fell off, the part we were in, that's why we got out, the front bit crashed into the cliff part up there and it burnt and I think they'll be dead, but in the back bit, some of them . . . we should try. Someone'll come to rescue us soon but until then it's only us and I don't know how long it'll stay on the rocks and if they can't get out they'll drown. Over there.'

She pointed. I looked. It was easier to do what she said. The alternative was to think for myself, and I felt too crap to do that.

Beyond the beach was a lagoon, and beyond that a reef. The tail section of the plane was resting on the reef, shifting under the breaking waves from the open sea. 'Most of the water's shallow, we can walk, we only have to swim the last bit, can you swim? I pulled you, after we crashed.'

I remembered floundering in shallow water, and someone pulling at my shirt, dragging me into the trees. 'You saved my life,' I said.

She blushed horribly and turned away. 'Maybe,' she mumbled. 'You might've been fine without me, anyway I hung on to you and it stopped me blowing away cos the wind was fierce, a huge wind, so you saved my life too . . . but we should go, quickly.'

I looked down at the figures on the beach. The girl was right, there were no adults. 'Don't waste time talking to them, it'll be all that squeaking and squealing and saying who we are, let's just GO,' she said even more emphatically than usual (she mostly spoke in capital letters). 'Come on, this way.'

I followed her: it was easier than arguing. She kept to the cover of the trees until we were as far from the others as we could be without going past the plane. Then she ran across the beach into the shallow water of the lagoon. I followed. We had to swim the last fifty yards, and when we started swimming I came back to myself. Breathe, stroke stroke, breathe, kick kick kick, the old routine, the safe routine. I got to the rocks much faster than she did and hauled myself up – sharp rocks, ouch.

I think that's when I really woke up. Not just to myself, but to all of it. The crash. The dead people. The possibility I'd be responsible for too much, that I wouldn't know the right thing to do.

I called back to warn her about cutting herself on the rocks, and to wait while I checked out the plane.

Then I forced myself to climb over the torn and tangled metal into the cabin. I was scared the wreck would shift and topple and drown me, and I was scared of the victims, mostly in case they weren't dead but dreadfully mutilated and I'd have to try to help them. I would, of course I would, but I'm squeamish and I've only got basic first aid.

It was bad enough. But at least the few remaining people strapped into their seats in the two rows at the front of the cabin were dead. Clearly dead. Broken, bloody and torn. I looked, looked away, looked back, behind the bodies across the empty rows to the seat I'd been in, at the very back.

The wreck was shifting as waves hit; the metal screamed. I panicked. It'll tilt and slip and I'll be stuck for ever, under water, with the bodies drifting past me, decomposing fingers in my hair . . .

Hysterical crap. Shock. But all the same, get out of here. I took a last look round and ducked out and away, back to the reef. Then I turned back. I was probably the last person ever to see them: some ceremony, some acknowledgement – 'Rest in peace,' I said. 'Good luck.'

Alice, 18, 5'8", mid-brown hair with red highlights: Hey, this isn't bad at all. The girls know my name, they've seen the ads, and three of them say they're fans. Way to go, Alice! One of them had a comb, s'well. No mirror yet and no make-up but I got started on the hair. Somebody's gotta come and get us sorted soon.

Wonderful winner: Rohini, 17
From: London, UK
Hair: black
Eyes: brown
Sibs: elder brother Mohandas, 21
Fave celebs: Franz Schubert
Wrote about: women in Hinduism
Cares about: clarity
***Uses: too right!* (lubricated tampon for medium to heavy flow)**

Nothing like nearly dying to make you glad to be alive. If I had the body, the fitness and the voice for it I'd lope down the beach singing 'Oh, What a Beautiful Morning'. As it is I admire my surroundings briefly. Best feature: parrots. Their voices are very like the other girls' (not good) but their plumage is bright, rich and various, not like the other girls (good). Worst feature: dwarfish, fleshy, spiky plants which sting my bum as I pee (v.bad).

Top practical feature, a big pool of water, very close. Seems OK. Not salt at all, tastes like expensive bottled water, of a rather delicious nothing.

Next issue, what to do. The beach is long, my legs short, the survivors scattered. Time for the rape alarm. The mountains could come to Kali.

Natural-history observation: parrots hate rape alarms. They all flap and squawk and flutter upwards in an explosion of non-formation flying. I cover my head, then uncover it, delighted by not being shat on. Which is taking the worthy behaviour of being grateful for small mercies to unheard-of lengths.

Euphoria. Which won't last long, I imagine, but while it lasts . . .

I step out onto the beach, look all the way down, to my right. A whole pack of them, undecided yet what to do, stirring but not moving, like a school of jellyfish. To my left, equally far away, just two. The tall blonde one and a smaller nondescript one, walking purposefully towards me. No adults at all.

Emma, 17, 5'10", blonde: I'd already started walking towards the clump of girls I could see, far down the other end of the beach. 'There really was no one I could've helped in the plane, was there,' said the girl, trotting beside me to keep up.

'Nobody at all,' I said.

'Good. Then it's not my fault. I thought they were dead when I got out, but the wind . . . I couldn't . . . and there was you, and I couldn't . . . Wait for me, don't go so fast . . .'

'We've got to talk to the other girls, see they're all right.'

'I don't want to,' said the girl.

'We've got to. Come on.'

'I'm afraid of girls,' said the girl. 'Can I say I'm with you? That I knew you before?'

'No point in lying,' I said. 'We don't have to lie. You're with me now all right. What's your name?'

'Anneka.'

'I'm Emma.' She'd stopped again. 'Do come on.'

It didn't look as many as twenty of them, and some were *very* young. All girls, all dressed the same: *I* was right. The only visible survivors were f' prizewinners' delegation for the conference. Disappointing I couldn't see the Indian girl, the only one I'd properly met, though I'd seen the others on the telly ads and the websites, of course.

I'd met her at the photo opportunity at Heathrow. We'd been lined up by gushing, metallic PR women in the VIP lounge, issued with our *right!* sweatshirts, chinos and trainers. We'd been photographed in front of the promotional stand. Then we'd been handed over to an amiable but distracted Australian woman in her twenties ('Call me Fliss') who'd been mostly worried about her baby which her husband or partner didn't seem able to stop crying, and her eyes had kept flickering across the lounge to the baby while she said all the right things about us being prizewinners and remarkable women (the youngest girls had giggled at this) and how we'd all enjoy the week in Australia and meeting the prizewinners from other countries and . . . but her eyes kept straying to the baby, who was red in the face and fretful.

'Revolting, really,' said the Indian girl next to me. A short, squat girl with heavy facial hair, nearly a moustache.

'A baby can't be revolting.'

'Do you have a censor in your brain that goes snip-snip?' said the Asian girl. 'Of course a baby can be revolting.'

'Well, not to its mother.'

'And am I its mother?'

I'd liked her right off, though I shushed her in case anyone heard. I looked forward to getting to know her. Maybe after a while I could suggest doing something about the moustache.

Now I couldn't see her in the group at the other end of the beach. I couldn't see Fliss, either, or the baby. Some of the girls were crying. Separately. The rest were chattering.

My head was really hurting. I needed a paracetamol, but fat chance, because it was obvious that all anyone had was what they stood up in, and I was in chinos and a sweatshirt and *right!* trainers, and lucky still to have the trainers, because the coral reef'd been sharp and otherwise my feet would've been cut to ribbons.

The sun was strong. I could feel the wet clothes drying on me and the beginning of a tingle on my forehead and the back of my neck. I've quick-tanning skin and it wasn't a worry yet but Anneka had very fair skin and freckles. I must remember that, deal with it quickly, once I'd spoken to the others.

I kept walking, realising how long the beach was. About a mile, probably. It was very heavy going in the soft white sand, and I had to pick my way around heaps of seaweed and corpses of peculiar seabirds and fish, with Anneka following.

Which is when I heard the screaming sound, like a car alarm, very close. A city sound, shockingly out of place here. There was a fluttering of wings from the trees and brightly coloured birds flapped upwards and away. The Asian girl stepped from the tangle of trees onto the beach just in front of me. 'Parrots,' she said. 'Aren't they beautiful? I know nothing about birds, wish I did. Sorry about the noise but I thought we ought to get everyone together, everyone who can walk, that is, we should organise a search, hi, I'm Rohini, it's a rape alarm.' She waved a small square object in my direction. 'Another blast coming up, cover your ears.'

I covered my ears: another blast. The still-distant figures on the beach had turned and were starting to move down towards us, and one or two other girls were coming out of the trees. Good thing Rohini seemed to want to take charge, cos I still wasn't thinking clearly.

I took a good look at her. She could have passed for mid-twenties, being so solid. She was in the **right!** sweatshirt and chinos, like me, but it didn't suit her. She had short, wide legs and a barrel body, but beautiful hair, very thick and shiny, twisted up in a faux-casual style which would have taken me hours, always supposing I could have managed it. Lucky I've got good blonde hair and a decent-shaped head, so I wear it short.

'How old are you?' I said.

'Seventeen,' said Rohini. 'You?'

'Seventeen.'

'And how many months?' said Anneka, who was hovering anxiously.

We both smiled. 'Six months,' I said.

'Ten months,' said Rohini.

'Oh,' said Anneka, disappointed, subsiding.

'You're the oldest,' I said, and actually felt relieved. Not that it mattered, of course. We were both far beyond month-counting. But still . . .

'Oh, bollocks to that,' said Rohini. 'Who cares? We'll

14

work together. We're women.' She was being sarky, but it was true as well, and a comforting thought.

She pointed at Anneka. 'She with you?'

'Yes,' said Anneka. 'She's my sister.'

'No,' I said. 'I told you, Anneka. You're with me, but no lies.'

One of the girls was running towards us, ahead of the moving group, finding the sand hard going, looking as if she wished she hadn't volunteered. She was fourteenish, slightly plump, and her blonde hair was too fine for its cut. Her face looked like a moon with fluff round it. She reached us, gasping, and bent down with her hands on her knees to get her breath. She too was wearing chinos and the *right!* sweatshirt, which I was getting good and tired of. I'd felt stupid advertising a sanitary towel to start with, and now I felt vicious. I wished I'd never won the damn competition. I wished I hadn't even entered. I wished I was still in my bed at home not having to get up and not having this bloody headache.

'Hi, I'm Vanessa,' gasped the plump girl. 'Alice sent me. Is there anything wrong? What was that alarm? Does anyone need help?'

'Which is Alice?' said Rohini.

Vanessa turned and pointed to the leading figure in the approaching group, now only a hundred yards away. 'That one.'

As soon as I saw Alice I knew why Vanessa was running her errands. I've changed schools enough, God knows. I like a quiet life so I've had to learn how to hack it with the queen bee in my year. Appease some, ward off some, cosy up to some. But first you had to spot them: the pace-setters, the genuinely powerful ones.

Alice was a queen bee.

She was tall, not as tall as me but about five-foot-eight, with low-slung well-fitting chinos and bare feet. She had a square face with a slightly jutting chin which she held high, almost aggressively. She had a great many very white teeth, hennaed mid-brown hair twisted up and clasped, spikily, at the top of her head, and mid-size, hazel, deep-set eyes. She looked more American than English to me, maybe because of the teeth, maybe because she had the kind of low fore-head and prominent jaw that Americans value more than the English do. She'd have been a huge success in my least-favourite educational institution, a Boston high school where the casual clothes the other girls wore cost more than my laptop. I got away with it because I was tall, blonde and British, and the best swimmer in the school, but it was touch and go at times. Alice would've fit right in. She was a star. She smiled very widely. She made walking in bare feet through fine sand look cool.

'Doesn't matter how old *we* are,' I said to Rohini. 'She's in charge. Good luck to her.'

'Umm,' said Rohini. 'D'you know what someone said the automatic disqualification for a politician should be?'

'No idea,' I said shortly. My family quote at me ceaselessly. Pa and Ma are professors and my sister's a pain-in-the-bum literary know-all. I think quoting is showing off, intimidation and mostly irrelevant.

'Eagerness to seek office,' said Rohini.

Alice, 18, 5'8", mid-brown hair with red high-lights: Two more prizewinners, shit. When I heard the alarm thing I thought it was adults, or maybe rescuers. At least these were older, my age. If it'd been all kids, someone'd have to do the work. What did we have here? The fat swotty Indian one and the keen swimming one. I gave them a big smile anyway. Here we are, I said, sweeping my hand round at my posse. Why did we have to come to you? I said. Co-operation, crucial. No hierarchical structures. That's what I wrote about for the prize.

It's obviously more sensible to meet here, said the Indian, it's the middle of the beach, central, there's a shady clearing back there, cut down on sunburn, also a stream, and –

I shut her off, bossy cow. OK, OK, here we are, I said. We've been getting to know each other, talking about our experiences of the crash, sharing our feelings, better than keeping them in, you know. Want to introduce yourselves, share your feelings with us? I'll start, I'm Alice, this is Debs.

Hi, Alice, hi, Debs, I'm Emma, said the keen one. Bad luck she hadn't died. If some of them did, it should've been her. Dads monitored the website hits for me and he said she was my only competition. I had the most hits, except she had more, and more telly ads. He said, Maybe she'll get an illness, or maybe she's got a crap personality. You're the one, Princess, you deserve it.

Not that she was great-looking or anything. Bit tall.

Wonderful woman of courage:
   Deborah, 16
From: Coventry, UK
Hair: blonde
Eyes: green
Sibs: Haydon 15, Ryan 13,
      Carla 10, Kimberley 6,
      Linsey 3, Jemma 1
Fave celebs: Eminem
Wrote about: her life looking after her family
Cares about: sussing it
Uses: too right! (lubricated tampon for medium to heavy flow)

Posh bitch Emma smiles at me and says hi Debs like she's queen of the world welcoming me to her place so long as I grovel. Her face pinches when she looks at me, what's wrong with my hair anyway, I can go blonde if I want to, just cos I wasn't born with it or a silver spoon wedged up my arse either like her. I keep stumm, won't waste words on her. I'm with Alice. I'm with Alice. She's Miss in, obvious. And I'm Miss Out except this time I'm not because this Miss in took to me and I'm with her. The bossy Paki tells us to move out of the sun, well she'd know, why doesn't she go back there? If we get off the beach the rescue planes won't see us. Alice snubs her, good one. But the Paki won't take it. They'll be following the plane's distress signal, surely, she says, and they'll see the plane on the reef, and we'll hear them, we can come out and wave, she says, full of herself, and Alice gives in, she shouldn't have, though she pulls an acid face. OK, she says, let's go inside. So we all follow the Paki like a sad oldies conga line into the trees.

CHAPTER TWO

Anneka, 11, 5'1", mousy hair: Made sense about not being in the sun. Rohini makes sense, she's not as nice as Emma but OK. She led us into a clearing place like a cathedral, with huge towering trees which filtered the light so it was green. It had a peaceful holy feeling, like York cathedral, one of my favourite places. Not cos I'm religious. My mum has no time for religion – no time for anything much, mostly not even me – and my granpa hates it, I've never listened when he explained why, but when I lived in York with my mum I often hung out in the cathedral. It beat the shopping precinct. Wasn't full of gangs of girls bullying me, for a start.

YUK, squealed a kid, really girly, BEETLES. We all looked where she pointed. There were rotting leaves on the ground, like a mat. When I looked, I could see crawly things. Slightly yuk, there *were* beetles.

Emma and Rohini and I kept still but otherwise a stupid stampede started towards the beach. We haven't any sunblock, one of them said, we can't stay out in that sun, we'll all get cancer.

The stampede broke up, some of them came back

in, some went faster out, they collided. One of the smaller ones (titless, my age, should have known better) fell over and started screaming BEETLES BEETLES BEETLES. The rape alarm went off again. I jumped. Everyone stopped dead. That's better, said Rohini. The fallen-over girl was picked up and dusted off by kids near her, though they didn't look happy, praps in case they were brushing not just leaf mould but beetles. I want my mum! she howled.

Belt up, ickle, said an older girl near her, the pretty one with tons of bright red frizzy hair, the way they all dye it and perm it in Year 10 but hers was real. Nice beetles, right, she said, friendly cuddly fuckin beetles, all right. Her accent was like a telly person, very strong, London I think.

Rohini, 17, 5'2", black hair: The redhead piles in with enviable street authority. They'd be squeaking and scattering still if she hadn't sorted them. Once the beetle question is temporarily resolved, the rest of them go back into the clearing, still looking round warily for other wildlife. At this rate mankind'll have conquered cancer and established colonies on Sirius B by the time we've exchanged names. At least (unexpectedly) Alice does something useful. 'Sit down,' she says, pointing to fallen tree trunks. 'Sit on those, OK, settle down.' Gradually, the younger ones do, jostling and budging up and making groups.

'We were getting to know each other,' she says. 'Introducing ourselves. Let's carry on.'

Less useful. I'd briefly hoped for purposeful action from her, but find only vanity and demagoguery. 'We could organise a search for survivors first. Then we can wallow around in ourselves if we want to,' I say.

Alice's grimace is definitely hostile. 'That's not very upbeat,' she says, 'not very feelgood. We're all still in shock, some of us are injured . . .'

Complaint seeps from several of the younger ones: 'My head hurts . . .', 'I've done my leg in . . .' Perching on the tree trunks, they brandish minor injuries like self-mutilated beggars.

'You're right, we should go and look,' says the redhead who'd taken a firm line on the beetles. She's sitting on the far end of a tree trunk away from the others, but not as if she's being excluded: by choice, more as if she's working out who it's worth while allying herself with.

'What does everyone think?' says Alice. 'What about you, Debs?'

Debs is standing just behind her. 'You're right, Alice,' she says.

'You're right Alice what?' says the redhead. 'What's Alice right about?'

'Who are you?' says Alice. 'Why don't you introduce yourself?'

The redhead stands up, sighing and rolling her eyes. 'Hi, I'm Nadia, I'm fourteen years old from Eltham in South London and I want to work with challenged kids and save the planet . . .'

Which lifts my heart. Street authority and irony too.

'I totally agree with you about the planet,' says the pink-faced plump girl who ran ahead of the others on the beach, doing Alice's bidding. She's standing in a linked-arm group of three, also behind Alice. 'I'm Vanessa and these are my friends Charlotte and Mei Lin –'

'And I agree with you about the challenged kids,' says Mei Lin. 'I'm Mei Lin, and we're all from Surrey –'

'And I want to start saving the planet by looking for injured people, right? Are you listening to me or what?' snaps Nadia. 'All this stuff about us was on the websites for months, wasn't it? So any of us who can read will have seen it. While we're blatting on about our hopes and fuckin aspirations, people are maybe dying, and we could find them. So who else is coming?'

'Me,' I say. 'But also –'

'Me,' says Emma.

'And me,' says Anneka.

'We need two groups,' I say. 'One to go as near as we can to the top of the mountain –'

'All the way up there?' wails one of the youngest, who's been sobbing steadily ever since I first spotted her.

'No way to the top of that . . .'

'I broke my nail . . .'

'– to find out as much as possible about where we are. And someone needs to organise –' I battle on.

'But I'm hungry. I want some Cocopops . . .'

'. . . Chocolate . . .'

'. . . McDonald's Happy Meal . . .'

'There's *no fast food,*' I snap, meaning to shut them up. Mistake. We plunge into a hailstorm of cataloguing and wailing, Pot Noodles, waah, Smarties, waah . . .

'Oh, shit,' says Nadia. 'Put your hand up if you're under fourteen, OK?'

The hands go up. Too many of them. Nadia counts out loud. 'Fourteen and over we got me, plus Alice, two, Rohini, three, the goody-goods six . . .'

'Who're you calling the goody-goods?' protests Vanessa.

'You and your mates from Surrey who want to save the planet, OK? Debs, seven, Emma, eight . . . That's it?'

'What's wrong with being under fourteen?' says a sassy kid I'd noticed immediately. She's all legs and nose and her expression shouts, *It's not my fault, it's yours, I never.* 'I'm Tamsin, and I say that's age . . . something . . .'

'Ageist?' I suggest.

'Yeah, nothing wrong with being young. The future belongs to the young, my mum says. She's an activist, and I'm one too. We believe in democracy and recycling and banning cars and GM foods and hunting. She says I can make up my own mind, I can do whatever I want to, because –'

'Because you throw a hissyfit if you don't get your own way, most likely,' says Nadia. 'Can we get on?'

'We're all equal here, OK, OK,' says Alice, taking the spotlight back. She probably believes she'd speedage and crumble to dust without it. Maybe she's right. Happy thought, I'll give it a try. 'Thanks for your contribution, Tamsin. So who's going up to the top of the mountain with Rohini?' (No way's it going to be her.)

'I'll go,' says Nadia.

'And me,' says Emma.

'And me,' says Anneka anxiously.

24

'Whoever stays with the children needs to organise −' I begin.

'Who're you calling children?' says Tamsin.

'I'll stay with Alice,' says Debs.

'So will we,' says Vanessa. 'Right?' (To her friends, who nod.)

'So if four of us go up the mountain to see if this place is inhabited − there could be a town the other side −'

'. . . with a McDonald's . . .'

'. . . a theme park . . .'

'. . . a shopping mall . . .'

'− with a telephone,' I say. 'And maybe a doctor.' I didn't expect it, but of course we should check.

'In your dreams,' says Tamsin. 'This is an island. With nobody on it but us and beetles.'

'YUK!'

'We must check, anyhow, and see if there are any survivors in the front of the plane −'

'That all burnt out,' says Mei Lin.

'We should check,' I repeat. 'But realistically, most survivors'll be near the beach. So all of you could divide up and walk the shoreline, see if you can find anyone.'

'We'll be rescued any minute, anyway,' says Alice, 'if we get out on the beach so the rescue people can see us. That's what *we'll* do. We'll make it easy for them to find us.'

'And collect some food,' I say.

'Food?' says Alice.

I wait for a second, expecting a food wish-list from the kids. Silence. Maybe they aren't following the finer points of the conversation. I go on. 'There's coconuts, anyway. If you get some of those down you can all eat, and save some for us when we come back —'

'I'm not eating that stuff,' says Tamsin. 'I want real food. Like Nutty Corners, Frubs . . .'

Now they've got it.

'. . . pot Noodles . . .'

'. . . toast and jam . . .'

'. . . strawberry yoghurt . . .'

'Those coconut things are high up. How do we get them?'

'Plus there's bananas and breadfruit,' I say, ignoring the younger ones. 'But they really need to be cooked or else we'll all get gut-rot. Does anyone have a light?'

'Me,' says Nadia, fishing in one of her trouser pockets, 'but it's been soaked, may not work.'

Click, click, shake, click. Everyone watches the tiny flame flicker to life.

'Yay! We got fire!' says Nadia.

'Got any cigs?' says Tamsin.

'Dream on,' says Nadia. 'Not for an ickle girlie.'

'Surely they'll bring real food when they rescue us,' says Alice.

'You won't need this, then,' says Nadia, putting the lighter away.

'It'd be good to eat something soon,' says Emma, agreeing with me and placating Alice with her tone of voice.

'OK, OK,' says Alice, stretching out her hand and waggling her fingers towards her palm for the lighter. 'We'll get food. *And* make a fire *and* cook. *And* look around the shoreline. *As well* as being on the beach for the rescuers.'

I've been told so often, by so many people, that I'm impatient and judgemental that I take special care not to be. But even a generous assessor would probably agree that the likelihood of Alice fulfilling any of her appointed tasks is zero. So, should I stay behind and try to organise a search on the beach? And if I try, will I succeed? Probably not.

I still feel guilty as we leave her to it.

Anneka, 11, 5'1", mousy hair: I felt scads better when we started out up the hill and left the other lot behind. It was obvious where we had to go because behind the pool, to the right, there was a built path of big stones, leading almost straight up. So there must of been people on the island once, strong people cos the stones'd be very heavy to move. Now there was moss all over them and plants between and some of the stones'd shifted a bit, but you could still see where to put your feet.

On each side of the path the trees and bushes were so thick you'd have to cut your way through them, and they were pressing in on us, sort of grabbing at us, I thought, but didn't want to think. They were also, like, breathing out wet air, like a blanket all over us as soon as we got up above the clear space round the pool. Nadia was in front and after about a hundred metres she stopped and we all looked back. We were quite a lot higher up cos it was so steep, but we couldn't see anything. Just whopping great plants, dark green, light green, splotchey red and yellow fruit things, huge leaves and ordinary leaves but none of them I could put a name to.

This isn't going to work, I said, we can't see.

Hello, Rohini called out. Hello, is anyone there?

We all listened but there were no people-noises, just trees and stuff rustling and cracking, and parrots squawking, and the bird-noises from the sea.

Then there was a people-sound – Caaan't, caaan't . . . Like a man's voice, but weird, like strangled, coming from . . . somewhere in the middle of the island, not the beach.

Hello, hello, called Emma. Where are you?

No answer.

It's a bird, said Rohini.

Caaan't, caaan't . . . No, it was a person, it was a person.

It's a bird, said Emma.

Yeah, said Nadia. They both sounded relieved. We'd all been standing stiff, trying to listen. We sort of shifted about, still half-listening. It stinks up here, said Nadia.

It did, it stank of Granpa's shed, with mushrooms and just a bit of the mouse that died in our attic, dark things. I was scared, suddenly, like stepping into a hole you hadn't seen. What was hiding in there, behind the crooked giant plants? What was watching us?

I took hold of Emma's hand. Emma squeezed back, but I could tell the way her skin pulled away for a moment that she thought I was a royal pain. Or maybe she was scared herself. I looked at their faces. I think they were all spooked. Like Granpa says, as if a goose had walked over your grave.

Look, bananas, said Emma, pointing.

I looked at the green bulgy things she was pointing at. They didn't look like bananas to me. They looked like monsters in a telly science fiction. Any minute now they'd wave their tentacles and start to move . . . Something went in my head. Mustn't cry, they'll hurt me if I cry. Don't show weakness, Granpa says, or women will pick on you and tear your heart out and eat it. That's one of the things he says that I believe from what's happened to me, myself.

Tesco bananas, said Nadia. Any minute now, the man from Tesco'll come and pick them and stick those stickers on, and ship them to England where they'll turn yellow and your mum'll buy them for your tea.

Nadia was all wrong about my mum shopping, but she meant well, and it made me feel better. So what're we doing, exactly, where're we going? I said.

We're going as high as we can to get a good view. To check if we're on an island, if it's inhabited, if we can see any local people or plane people, said Rohini.

So it doesn't matter that we can't see while we're on the path, I said, but we call out as we go in case people can hear us.

That's right, said Nadia.

OK, then, I like things to make sense, I said.

Emma, 17, 5'10", blonde hair: It took us over two hours to reach the top of the path. No one answered our calls, and we called a lot to give us an excuse to stop because it was so steep. At one of our pauses Rohini insisted on weaving a leaf-hat for Anneka, and when Anneka refused to be the only one looking silly, she and I and Nadia made hats for all of us. Nadia's was easily the best design. The hat looked OK on me but Nadia's couldn't sit right on her mass of red hair: however she wore it, we laughed. Nadia took it cheerfully. 'If I had a mirror I'd show you lot. Jungle fashions are hot on the street right now.' (I expect she knew they weren't as well as I did.)

Plodding up, I had too much time to think, and mostly what I thought was what a fool I was to be here. The whole competition thing had been stupid enough to start with. I'd seen it advertised, dismissed it as a transparent rip-off. But Mrs Wagstaffe made us write on the set topics as part of the A Level exam coursework, and then bullied me to enter. 'Yours is *such* a persuasive piece, Emma, limpid with hope. A winner for certain . . .'

'Limpid with hope.' Yuk. Like it was soaked in body fluids. Why'd I agreed? I'd been sure I wouldn't win, and I'd wanted to stop Wagstaffe going on and on at me, foaming at the mouth with eagerness and spraying me with spittle. '*So* important for women to reflect on being women, *such* a good idea for young women to join together in harmony discussing gender issues, *such* fun to meet the other prizewinners and visit Australia and the **right woman!** theme park . . .'

Weird how Wagstaffe got to be middle-aged without leaving the egg. How come she couldn't see the whole deal for the barefaced marketing promotion it obviously was? How come she was the only person in the western world not to see through Ken Wright, Canadian multi-millionaire entrepreneur, with his perma-tan and hair transplants and toothcapped grin? Since when was he likely to give a toss about gender issues?

Look at it from his point of view; it was a sweet deal. He launches a range of feminine hygiene products (yuk), announces the competition (publicity) and then pays off the prizes in kind: a flight to Australia on his cut-price airline, accommodation and food at one of his middle-range hotels, entrance to his theme park, all of which tacky products get publicity. Plus he gets thirty prizewinners, 11–18, who he uses in television ads worldwide and plasters all over his trashy website.

I had to stop beating myself up, I thought. So I'd been stupid to enter, even stupider to agree to come on the victory trip. But here I was and here we were and –

'AAAAAAAAAAAH!' screamed Anneka, and vanished, her voice silenced in mid-scream. She'd just stepped off the path to pee, she was no distance away, but one second she'd been there, squatting, the next she wasn't. Nadia and I both started to move towards where she'd been, but Rohini put her arms across to bar our way.

'Wait,' said Rohini. 'You don't want to go down too . . . Anneka? Anneka?'

We were all stretching, peering, but all we could see was foliage.

'Anneka? Anneka? Anneka?' We were all calling now.

'Shut up,' said Rohini. 'Let her answer.'

We listened. The usual island noises, creaking trees, the plop-plop-plop of water dripping, the far-off cries of birds, behind it all the heavy roll of the sea. No Anneka.

I went to move again; Rohini stopped me again. 'Anneka, is that you? Speak up! Louder!'

Rohini must've heard something I hadn't. I listened even harder. There was just a murmur, a breath of words. Not far away. At least she hadn't fallen down a deep hole, which is what I'd feared. 'You've got to speak *louder!*' said Rohini.

'. . . don't want to . . . them . . .'

'*What?*'

'Their place . . . don't want to . . .'

Rohini touched my arm. 'You talk to her. She's your puppy,' she whispered.

'Anneka? This is Emma. Come on, please, you've got to talk louder, tell us where you are, and *don't move.*'

'Their place, all the men . . . rude . . . mustn't shout . . .'

What *was* she talking about? Was that rude as in obscene, or rude as in impolite? 'Is there a man there?' I said.

'Lots of them,' she said, just a bit louder.

'How many?'

'Eight . . . nine . . .'

'Where are you, Anneka?' said Rohini.

'House. Stone house. Just down, not far.'

'How far? Are you hurt?'

'Not hurt. Not far.' Now her voice was clearer I could tell it was tight, with shock or fear.

'Will the men talk to you, Anneka?' said Rohini.

'Can't . . . very old . . . just heads . . . on poles . . .'

'Eeeuch,' said Nadia under her breath. 'Poor kid. Rotting heads.'

I climbed down to get her, carefully, holding on to a trailing creeper for support. When I landed, I saw why she'd been quiet. She was hunched up, her back pressed against a disintegrating stone wall. Opposite, only a few feet away, were two rows of stakes topped by skulls. The stakes were tilting away from each other. One was leaning directly forward, almost parallel to the ground so the skull was inches from her. Dotted round the skulls were shells and the remains of pots. If I hadn't had to look after her I'd've been scared too. 'OK,' I said. 'Here we go, come on,' and I pulled her out.

She was very, very quiet for the next few minutes. 'So what is it? What were they?' she kept whispering. Rohini made us keep going up, and she kept repeating, 'It's OK, Anneka, it was a skull shrine. How they buried important people. To give them respect. Like we used to in a tomb in a graveyard.'

Rohini was going first, Anneka next. Nadia and I made faces at each other. I don't know what she felt, but I felt like I'd just had the ground fall away from my feet, like Anneka. I'd sort of thought the island was just a place we happened to be staying in, like a badly equipped motel. Now it seemed to have a life of its own. I didn't know whether what Rohini was telling Anneka was true or just a good invention. I didn't know if the people who'd built the skull house were still here, or if not them, their descendants. I didn't know what they'd done, long ago, or maybe not so long ago, with the bodies that had carried the heads.

CHAPTER THREE

Rohini was first to reach the clearing at the path's end. Nadia was struggling behind her, and I was at the back going steady, with a shattered Anneka on my shoulders. I was easily the fittest – hardly surprising as the others weren't in training for anything I don't suppose – but my headache had come back.

'I'd kill for a paracetamol,' I said and dumped Anneka in a heap on the ground.

'Look,' said Rohini. 'Just look.'

We did and it silenced us. We weren't on the highest point of it, but we were far enough up to confirm that it was an island. I'd known it really but I was still heart-sinkingly disappointed.

Rohini pointed. 'A volcano,' she said. Across a shallow valley there was a towering blackish-greyish shape.

'I hope it's dormant,' I said.

'Shit, it's hot,' said Nadia. 'But less sticky than down there. Bit of air.'

Understatement. It was windy. Anneka leant into the wind and let it support her, arms outstretched. 'It's drying me,' she said, really pleased, then scrabbled after her flying hat, right to the edge of a sheer drop. We all grabbed for her but Nadia got her first, then stamped on the hat.

'Sorry,' said Anneka.

'So you ought to be,' said Nadia. 'Stupid little cow.'

They grinned at each other, and Nadia gave her a slap on the backside with one hand, offered her the hat with the other. She's good with kids, I thought. Great, that'll take the pressure off me.

I looked away from the volcano at the coast the other side from our beach. There was no sand, all rocks, and no protecting reef, so the waves broke hard and high. Any rescue by boat would have to come in our side.

'A volcanic island with a coral reef,' said Rohini. 'Somewhere between Honolulu and Canberra.' She lowered her voice so Anneka couldn't hear. 'That's plenty of space to be lost in.'

'Oh, surely they'll find us,' I said. 'They'll know where the plane was when it crashed. They'll have it on radar or whatever. And the black box thing planes carry . . . and satellite photographs . . . the Americans have everything on satellite photographs . . .'

'Um,' said Rohini.

Until that moment I'd been absolutely certain that rescue was, at the most, hours away. But, moustache or not, Rohini'd made sense so far. 'You don't agree?' I said.

'I don't know. It's been hours since the storm dropped. They'd be here by now. If they knew where we were.'

'They're just delayed,' I said. The alternative was . . . was . . . I wouldn't even voice it.

'Ever read *Lord of the Flies*?' said Rohini.

'Of course. Set book, year ten. And . . . ?'

'Same situation.'

'Different gender.'

'What're you talking about?' said Anneka, dancing between us.

Change the subject. 'We can't see anybody,' I said. 'No smoke from fires, no paths much, no houses. It's an uninhabited island . . .'

'Except for us,' said Anneka pointing down. You could see the beach, far below, and the tiny figures of the other girls, mostly bunched together. 'But I can't see our fire, either, and we asked them to make a fire, didn't we, and they took your lighter, Nadia, and they haven't made a fire, typical −'

'Maybe they have made a fire and we can't see it,' I said.

'Typical of what?' said Rohini

'Typical of that Alice, selfish and thoughtless,' said Anneka.

'Selfish and thoughtless,' mimicked Nadia. 'You're perfect, I s'pose?'

'Look, the front of the plane,' said Rohini, pointing at a burnt swath in the thick vegetation of the valley.

'Oh,' said Anneka, sobered. 'Oh. They'll all be dead in that, won't they? Ought we to go down and look?'

'No,' the rest of us chorused.

'That's all right then,' said Anneka.

Anneka, 11, 5'1", mousy hair: It was quicker coming down than going up, but even so it took a long time. I was hot and hungry and very tired. I couldn't have managed if Emma hadn't carried me the last bit and I felt bad about it because she was tired too, we all were.

It was great when we got to the bottom and went into the clearing. Someone had cleaned it all up and arranged the logs like benches in a half-circle facing the pool and swept the rotting leaves away down to clean sand and put empty coconut shells neatly by the pool. It was like coming to a strange home, and I cheered up right away. So did the others, I could see.

Vanessa, Charlotte and Mei Lin came running into the clearing, all talking at once. We could see you coming down the hill, we knew you were nearly here, wanted to surprise you, doesn't it look good, looks much better, a meeting place for us, for when the rescuers come, we can give them food, come out on the beach, look, look, we've got the fire going, it took us ages because we had to dry the wood but we made it with stones and then we baked the breadfruit, and it burnt, so we threw it away then we wrapped the next lot in leaves, and it doesn't taste bad now, and look we've opened some coconuts for you and we've collected lots of shells to put the milk in, and the shells for the water of course . . .

The fire was a little way out on the beach and the flames burnt so bright and clear you could hardly see them in the sun. They'd built it on a bed of stones, square and solid. It was too hot to go right up to but we kept back and admired it.

You must be exhausted, said Mei Lin. Sit down, sit down here, we'll get you food and water . . .

Water and food, said Vanessa.

We went back inside the trees and sat on the logs and they brought us water and four vegetable things wrapped in leaves.

Nadia spat hers out. Blek, she said, that's blek, I can't eat that.

You may have to, said Rohini. I like breadfruit, anyway, you get used to it.

I like it a lot, I said to be polite. It's weird but good.

Me too, said Emma, but I think she was lying like me to cheer them up. She was kind of choking on it but she kept lying through her choke, mmm, delicious.

This is excellent, said Rohini, and very well cooked.

Really, said Charlotte.

Really really, choked Emma.

Really really, I said as well, trying to take my mind off the taste by looking at the goody-goods (mustn't call them that), the three friends, to make sure I could name them apart. I'm good with names but even so it'd be easy to think of them as a lump and I bet everyone did and it wouldn't be fair. Vanessa was the tall blonde round-faced one, Charlotte shorter, only my height, and more sort of wiry, with tanned skin and grey eyes and a bony nose, Mei Lin was taller than me, skinny like me, and easy to tell cos she was Chinese.

Did you find anything? Vanessa said.

Nobody said anything at first. I hoped they wouldn't say about the skull place I'd fallen into, cos it might

38

worry the three friends, plus I didn't want to remember it.

No. It's definitely an island, said Nadia.

So there's no one else on it? said Vanessa.

As far as we could see, nobody else on it, said Rohini, and no other survivors. Did you find any down here?

Two more people turned up, Rouchelle and Tawheeda, Vanessa said.

How old? I said.

Bout fifteen, give or take, she said.

But we didn't acksherly *find* anyone, said Charlotte, cross. Even when we heard the man calling in the jungle . . .

A man? What man? said Nadia.

He was screaming can't can't like he was in pain, said Vanessa, like he needed help *right then*, and we'd have gone –

But Alice told us, we three had to do the cooking and the fire . . .

. . . and collect the food, and we did . . .

. . . and Debs was supposed to organise the search party with the younger ones, but she didn't . . .

. . . cos the younger ones wouldn't do it, they wanted to play, and then they went swimming, most of them, and they just wouldn't do what they were told, and just messed around and played . . .

. . . until . . . Charlotte started, then she stopped. The other two looked at each other. Something was up.

I don't think the sound you heard was a person, said Rohini. We heard it too, and we thought it was a bird, so don't worry about it.

39

But there could be other people, said Mei Lin, and . . . and no one's come to rescue *us* yet.

And there was a thudding, scary silence. I moved closer to Emma.

Maybe . . . Emma began, and stopped.

Maybe they're not coming, said Charlotte.

When she said it, the words kind of dropped like a hot iron on my foot (I know cos Mum dropped one on me once) and I shunted up even closer to Emma.

Alice said they'd come, said Vanessa.

We all thought they would, said Emma.

Being fair, I reckon, though why she should stand up for Alice –

And they will, said Rohini. Meanwhile we'd better assume nobody'll come till tomorrow at least, and get organised for the night.

The night? said Mei Lin. What about it?

Maybe we should sleep near the fire, to keep insects and snakes away, plus the younger ones might be frightened when it gets dark. And we could dig a latrine.

I hate the dark, said Nadia, It's never dark at home in Eltham, not proper dark, always streetlights. I like streetlights.

There was another thudding silence. I don't know what the others were thinking but I missed Granpa and our bacon-and-egg suppers. Lucky I like bacon and egg because that's what he mostly cooks. I budged up even closer to Emma to get away from the fear that was all around us. I tried not to say anything but I did, it just came out. I want my granpa.

Emma hugged me and Nadia said, Listen, ickle, it'll be fine. You'll see your granpa soon.

Where? I said.

Back home.

But I want to go to Australia, that was the prize, to go to Australia, I want to go to the theme park. I want . . . I sounded like a spoilt brat but I couldn't stop, not even when I wasn't making sense, because I couldn't care less about the theme park, I don't know why I said it.

You will, said Emma. What'll happen is, they'll take us to Australia when they rescue us.

I don't want to go straight back home. I want my granpa in Australia.

That's what'll probably happen, said Nadia. They'll fly our relatives out. With the publicity and all, they'll be all over us. And they'll be searching for us right now, with everything they've got.

I made a ginormous effort to stop crying and blew my nose on a leaf. I had to get away and stop annoying them. Going to wee, I said, and went off into the trees, anywhere they couldn't see me.

Rohini, 17, 5'2", black hair: With Anneka gone, I dive right in. 'What's the "until"?' I say. 'Charlotte? What's the "until" about, that none of you would go on with?'

The goody-goods look at each other and look away.

'Get on with it,' says Nadia.

They go into their taking-tums-to-talk routine.

'Suitcases. They found suitcases washed up, and we said they shouldn't be opened but kept for the people who owned them. They're dead of course but still they don't belong to us. We all said that, and Alice said that at first, but then they started opening them anyway when we went away and throwing everything about, it was such a mess, and Debs said we couldn't stop them and she wasn't going to try. That's because she wanted some of the stuff herself, and then she gave the best stuff to Alice and started dressing her up like a queen with the jewels and we found the jewels in a locked case. Vanessa opened the locked case, she shouldn't have, well they were being so feeble about it, you shouldn't have, no I shouldn't really, anyway once Debs dressed Alice up she looked great, no she didn't she looked stupid, no she looked frightening, no she didn't she looked great, specially with the make-up, then they all took the make-up and the best clothes, there was some great gear, they shouldn't have taken it, we didn't, we didn't, we didn't . . .'

'Chill out, OK?' says Nadia. 'Then what?'

'Then they left it all, left it scattered everywhere, such a waste, not ours, such a mess, shouldn't have, so we came back and finished here . . .'

'You've done a great job,' says Emma.

'And?' I say, because they haven't finished, there's still an unspoken in the air.

They look at each other again.

'Get on with it,' says Nadia.

'Then we heard the noise, like chanting, it was weird, no it was just like a chant, I didn't like it anyway, no I know, so we went to look, and they were dancing and chanting *Another one bites the dust* over and over, and stamping, it's only the Queen number, well I've never heard it, well I have it was on 'Gladiators', really really old, so we came back and made more bread-fruit for you, *they* didn't even look at their breadfruit, they just threw it down and stamped on it . . . And we're glad you're back.'

The goody-goods're overreacting. Stealing from the suitcases, dressing up, it's annoying of course, but just the kind of thing children do. I'd found being a child almost unendurable at times because one was always being expected to join in songs, dances, ludicrous games. And even worse than taking part in them, one was expected to enjoy them. But it was tiresome and purposeless more than frightening.

'So *we'll* get on with the survivor-search, then,' says Emma briskly. The goody-goods are obviously relieved. I'm not. Mental activity is far more congenial to me than physical, and we've already been up the hill.

'OK,' says Nadia, wearily, no keener than I am. 'Hey, listen.'

Approaching voices, singing. *Tell me what you want, what you really really want . . . ziggy ziggy oooo . . .*

Emma, 17, 5'10", blonde hair: They sounded happy. We went out onto the beach to watch them come, shuffling and prancing and chanting. They weren't great at holding the tune. but they all had the words, *This I swear, and all I want from you is the promise you'll be there* . . . except for an ickle right at the front who hadn't got with the programme but was being a pony, *clipclop, clipclop, nnyyyehhh.* The ickles were in Hallowe'en gear, all different clothes and painted faces.

43

Alice, right at the back with Debs, looked amazing. Her face was made up, not painted. She was in a tiny bustier, black leather bikini bottoms, a thick diamante choker and chains of diamante body jewellery. Breathtaking.

'Warrior queen, know what I mean,' called Nadia. 'Looks great, Alice.'

'Looks great,' I echoed, cos it did. Wouldn't have looked bad on me either, specially as I have a longer neck.

'Looks really really *silly*,' whispered Anneka, right behind me.

'Miaow miaow,' said Nadia.

'What about *me*?' said Tamsin, dancing in front of us. '*Giving you everything, all that love can bring . . .*' She'd painted a cat-face. It suited her.

'Miaow miaow,' said Nadia again, making cat-claws at her.

'Hisssss,' said Tamsin, making cat-claws back. They both grinned and Tamsin danced away.

'Find anyone?' said Debs. 'We found two.' She was in the same gear as Alice, give or take a few chains, but her body was scrawny and her skin pale and blotchy so she looked foolish, like a sad guest on a TV talk-show with a caption 'Debs – dresses to please herself'.

'No, we didn't,' I said quickly before Rohini could respond to the one-up challenge of Debs's tone. 'Come and sit down. Let's talk.'

'Glad to,' said Alice. 'I'm shattered.'

In the clearing, the goody-goods were standing round looking sheepish.

'Haven't they done a great job?' I said.

'Yeah,' said Debs. 'We seen it already.'

'Thanks, guys,' said Alice. 'Brilliant. Sorry you missed out on the gear. There's plenty left if you all want to get some.'

The goody-goods looked at each other. Vanessa cracked first. 'Thanks, Alice,' she said.

'Thought you was too good for it,' said Debs.

'Wasn't ours, didn't belong to us, didn't think we should . . .' Charlotte and Mei Lin ground to a halt.

'No way to stop the kids,' said Debs.

'There really wasn't,' said Alice.

'It must've been difficult,' I said.

'Yeah,' said Nadia. 'What's done's done. We'll go get something later.'

Alice sat down, Debs beside her. 'I'd kill for some water,' she said. Vanessa fetched it while the rest of us sat down on a log opposite. 'No rescue yet,' she said, and let all the unspokens hang in the air.

'Maybe we'd better assume they're not coming,' said Rohini.

'*Not coming*!' said Alice. 'What d'you mean?'

'I mean make plans as if they're not coming, worst-case-scenario plans.'

'Won't happen,' said Debs.

'What won't happen?' snapped Rohini.

'They'll come all right,' said Debs.

'Let's have a meeting,' said Alice. 'Talk about it.'

'Better if we sort out what we need to do first. Without upsetting the younger ones,' I said quickly.

'We're all equal,' said Alice. 'Just because they're younger –'

'You talk such rubbish,' said Rohini.

45

'We've got to work together,' said Alice. 'All of us. No hierarchical structures.'

'We don't want to frighten them,' I said.

Rohini, annoyed, purple in the face, went steamrollering on. 'We're older. We know more than they do. Hierarchical structures have nothing to do with it, as you'd know if you weren't just parroting some load of crap you downloaded from the Net –'

'That's what won my prize,' said Alice blankly.

'Which doesn't mean it isn't a load of crap,' said Nadia. 'Lots of them were.'

'Well, mine wasn't,' snapped Alice. 'The Net's brilliant. You got the Net, you got the know-how.'

'Pity you can't download a brain,' said Rohini.

Alice glared. 'And what's to sort out?'

'Everything,' said Rohini. 'Food, warmth, health, hygiene, organisation, morale, and looking for injured survivors. Which you should've done in the first place while we went up the sodding hill.'

I got up and walked away from the logs to break the tension. 'This isn't helping,' I said. 'Everyone's fed up, OK? And uncomfortable, I bet. I've got a headache from the crash and blisters on my feet from the climb and sore patches all over my body where my clothes have rubbed from the salt –'

'It's doing my head in,' said Nadia. 'Baffling my brain. What if nobody comes for us? Ever?'

'Then we stay here,' said Rohini. 'But at least we can stay here as safely and comfortably as possible.'

'Which means we've got to work together,' said Alice triumphantly. 'That's what I said. We should have a meeting, and discuss it.'

'The meeting comes *after* we decide what to say at the meeting,' said Rohini. 'That's how you run them.'

'That's not how it is,' said Alice. 'Open. Everything's got to be open.'

'Including dead people's suitcases,' Rohini snapped. They glared at each other. Rohini was the first to look away. 'You're so vain and stupid,' she said flatly. 'It's hopeless.'

Huge mistake. She'd gone too far. The goody-goods gasped, outraged, and my irritation with Alice immediately refocused on Rohini, who should have known better.

Alice lowered her eyes. 'I'm sorry you think so,' she said bravely. 'I'm only trying to do my best. I'm sure we all are. I'll call the meeting. Give me the alarm thing, I'll let it off.'

'No you won't, it's mine.'

'What does it matter who does it?'

'If it doesn't matter, then why shouldn't I do it? It's mine anyway.'

'Oh, cut the crap,' said Nadia, taking the alarm and sounding it.

Immediately, the younger ones started piling in, with two slightly older black girls at the back. I hadn't seen them before.

No one commented on the transformation of the clearing, but they settled themselves on the logs quickly, probably influenced, though they didn't know it, by the goody-goods' tidy half-circle. They mostly looked overtired and ratty, and quite badly sunburnt.

Alice stood in the centre, bravely. Annoying girl:

47

what'd *she* got to be brave about particularly? Debs
stood at her elbow, just behind her.

'Hi there!' said Alice. 'Welcome. Special welcome
to Rouchelle and Tawheeda, cos they weren't at the
first meeting so they haven't met all of us. Want to
introduce yourselves?'

The newcomers pressed their heads together, whispered, and lapsed into silence.

'Come on, we all want to get to know you,' said
Alice. 'Don't you want to tell us about yourselves?'

The newcomers whispered again, then the tall thin
one spoke. 'Not speshly,' she said.

'C'mon,' snapped Debs. 'We all had to. Gerron with
it.'

'I'm Emma,' I said encouragingly.

'Hi,' said the shorter newcomer, making the best of
it. 'I'm Rouchelle and this is Tawheeda, we're mates,
from London, and . . .' She tailed off. 'What else d'you
want me to say?'

'You're fifteen, right?' said Anneka.

'Sixteen.'

'Oh, good.'

'Where in London?' said Nadia, probably hoping
for Eltham.

'Kilburn,' said Tawheeda.

'Eltham, me,' said Nadia.

'Right,' said Rouchelle.

'So, hi everyone,' said Tawheeda.

'Hi . . .'

'Hi . . .'

'Hi . . .'

'When can we go home?'

48

'My foot hurts . . .'

'I'm sunburnt . . .'

'Cannava drink?'

'I feel sick . . .'

'Did you find the man?'

'Cannava drink that isn't water?'

'What did you say?' said Rohini fiercely.

'Cannava drink that isn't −'

'No, not you − *you*,' said Rohini, zeroing in on the spindly kid who'd mentioned a man. 'What did you say?'

'I never,' said the girl helplessly, looking round for reassurance.

'Don't bully her,' said Alice triumphantly.

I was instinctively on Rohini's side (a man?), but really pissed off with her lack of people-skills. How come she couldn't see that in Alice's climate she had to talk to the younger ones sickly sweet, like a kids' TV presenter? Nadia rolled her eyes at me, then went over, squatted down in front of the girl (who'd now decided to cry and was gaining popular support) and took her hand. 'Hey. No need to cry. What's your name? Come on, smile. You've got a great smile − yes you have. What's your name?'

'Rosie.'

'What a cool name. Rosie, tell us, what were you saying about a man?'

'Did anyone find him?'

'You lot were supposed to be the ones looking,' said Rohini.

'No we weren't,' snapped Tamsin.

'Yes you were,' chorused the goody-goods.

49

'Hey, now, guys,' said Alice, 'let's not get into the blame thing here.'

'Tell us about the man, Rosie,' said Nadia. 'When did you see him?'

'When we got out of the plane . . . I don't want to talk about it, it was scary . . .' She fell back into tears.

'Let her alone,' said Tamsin.

'Scary how?' said Alice. 'Did he make you do nasty things?'

'Pedo,' said Tamsin with contempt. 'My mum says . . .'

'Pedo, yuk!'

'Pedo, yuk!'

The younger ones leapt up from the logs and scurried about.

A short blast of Rohini's rape alarm stopped them. 'Sit *down*!' she said.

Sulkily, they did.

'Please,' said Rohini. 'We need to know. If this man is injured, we must find him quickly.'

'But he's a pedo,' said Tamsin. 'He hurt Rosie. We shouldn't help him, he doesn't deserve it. Pedos are the pits, my mum says, nail em to a tree by their bollocks, that'll teach them . . .'

'Hush, Tamsin,' said Nadia. 'You're upsetting Rosie. She wants to help, don't you, Rosie? You want to save lives, don't you? We all do, don't we? And he wasn't a pedo, was he, Rosie?'

Hypnotised, Rosie shook her head.

'Why was he scary?'

'Old and ugly and bleeding and scary . . .'

'So when did you see him? Right after the crash?'

Rosie nodded her head.

'On the beach?'

Nod.

'Then where did he go? Into the trees?'

Nod.

'Where?'

She pointed, vaguely.

'Can you show us? Now?'

'Cannava drink that isn't water?'

'No,' snapped Rohini.

'What about the baby?' said a voice. It was the ickle who'd been more comfortable as a pony than a Spice Girl. 'The man'll be OK, speshly if he's a pedo. But the baby . . .'

CHAPTER FOUR

Rohini, 17, 5'2", black hair: Just when I thought things couldn't get any stupider . . . Obviously, we *all* have to search for the baby and the man, if they exist. Equally obviously, it isn't going to happen. Quite a few of the younger ones won't look alone (split up, spread out, no way) in case they find the man (pedo! – on no evidence at all, that I can see). The baby's a more popular victim (aaahhh), though when I suggest that they get off their backsides instead of just aaahing I'm shouted at and frowned down.

It ends up with Emma, Nadia, the goody-goods, Anneka and me, plus the kid who claimed to have heard the baby. Everyone else stays behind to comfort the kid who saw the man.

It's getting dark. We look for the baby first. Emma finds him. Baby alive (just). Mother, Fliss the Flustered who was nominally in charge of us, dead. In a tangle of bushes just feet in from the beach.

By then it's dark. We send the goody-goods (aahing for Europe), with the baby, back to the rest of the party. Between them they can manage something.

Debs at least (judging from her website) has plenty of experience with babies.

Emma, Nadia, Anneka and I scoop away enough sand with our bare hands to bury and cover Fliss's body. Rigor's set in, so we don't have to feel guilty about not giving CPR. I feel bad about us not finding them earlier. I'd tried to get a search organised, but 'I tried' is always an indictment. I should have succeeded. I've always lacked polloi-skills. I've never seriously intended to acquire them – fatal flaw, arrogance, smack hands Rohini.

When the burial's over, Emma organises us into collecting some of the stuff scattered round the plundered suitcases, since we're up that end of the beach. None of us want to, but Emma insists that we'll all need stuff to sleep on and cover ourselves with. So we put on as many layers as we can of warmish clothing, and carry as much as we can.

When we get back, the others squabble over the best sleeping-wraps (of course). I take mine (by no means the best, but not the worst either), dig away in the sand to make a hip-hole, and go to sleep. They can get on with it.

Anneka, 11, 5'1", mousy hair: I don't know why, but I didn't like it when Rohini went to sleep. Emma was still awake, after all. But somehow with Rohini gone it was like a lighthouse had gone out, no more flashing light, whew-round, whew-round. Not that you always wanted the light but it was comforting because she was thinking and you sort of felt while she was thinking she'd think of everything so you didn't have to. I thought she was half-sulking, too, or upset with herself, or something.

Debs was really good with the baby. She washed it and made a nappy from tearing up a cotton caftan. It was a boy, about eight months old, she reckoned. She quietened it down just by holding it, and she fed it, sucking from her fingers dipped in coconut milk. The kids liked it while she had it because it was quiet, but before that it was handed round and fussed over and it wailed and wailed. No wonder. Any normal person hates being squeaked at and messed about, let alone a shocked baby that had just lost its mother, but catch them understanding that.

Then Debs wanted to give it to Emma to look after but the baby cried when Emma took it and Alice was sort of triumphant, saying only Debs can look after it (her Debs, who she sort of owns) and that's what it came out at, Debs was to look after it so Alice owned the baby that all the kids wanted. If Emma'd had a bit longer the baby would have stopped crying and known it was on to a good thing. Babies aren't stupid, I think, just slow to get it in a new situation. Which you can't blame them for.

Then the kids started to go to sleep, wrapping themselves up in the stuff we'd brought from the suitcases, soft fluffy big things Emma called pashminas and beach dress things and towels. It wasn't cold at all, just a little cooler than being in the shade during the day, but they took the stuff and curled up, the really silly ones with their thumbs in their mouths.

Bit unfair to say silly. I pick my scabs when I'm stressed, and I was picking my scabs then, watching the three friends topping up the fire. I would've helped, cept they looked proud, as if they owned the fire, and I thought to offer would be one of those unhelpful helps that people do all the time, mostly to be mean, I think, sometimes cos they haven't worked out how it gets on your nerves. The one that really drives me mad is when I've been bullied or I'm upset in a group and trying not to be noticed, and then someone says oh Anneka are you upset and then everyone looks at you. So I let the three friends get on with the fire (which was now really really hot).

Emma was talking with the older ones. I wanted her to go to sleep but she wasn't going to. They'd settled in, talking, with those sort of low voices, almost whispers, which mean they were enjoying themselves and they didn't want to be intruded on, and her back was turned to me.

I didn't think I'd sleep but I took two large towels and picked myself somewhere near where the trees came over the beach, cos I don't mind insects and I wanted to be able to slip away without disturbing anyone if I needed to wander round at night, which I do sometimes when I can't sleep, which I sometimes can't. The best scenario of course would be to be right beside Emma, but that wasn't going to happen for a while and I didn't want to annoy her. Couldn't afford to.

Debs, 16, 5'5", dyed blonde hair: So there I was again, holding the baby, back to square one – in the top place, though, with Alice. She and posh-bitch Emma and the full-of-herself redhead who's weird

55

somehow tho I haven't sussed how yet, just not right, all talking about themselves and their lives and who'd be missing them, and now and then laughing, and Emma'd turn to me and offer to take the baby, and I'd've let her, boy would I, but Alice sees through her, knows she doesn't mean it, knows I'm the best one, Alice knows it, Alice knows . . . Doesn't know the work, tho, she doesn't know the work of a baby, how it goes on and on every minute and it's your life gone, swallowed up down a black hole and just when you think it's asleep it wakes and yowls and you want to stuff a nappy down its throat just to shut it up, and I can't join in now to the chat about homes and lives because if I talked it'd wake the baby. And maybe also cos I don't know what to say.

Alice, 18, 5'8", mid-brown hair with red highlights: The wind-down was excellent. I looked great and everyone knew it. The goody-goods fetched water and more coconut and the best pashminas for my sleeping gear and did the fire. The fat swotty Indian'd gone to sleep so the GBH-of-the-ear-hole quotient went right down. No more stupid lists of things we hadn't had time to get round to, 'sif we can do everything. 'Sif we should, just dumped out here with no one to look out for us.

I told Emma about Dads and how he'd go ballistic when he knew I was missing. No one's ever going to hurt my princess, he always says, not while there's breath in my body. And I told about the time I got bad marks in my GCSEs and he said he's sue the exam board. Mum kept on at him not to and he didn't, which was good as well cos exams don't matter and we saved the lawyers' fees and spent some of the money on coaching for my A Levels, which helped a lot with the coursework.

Emma and Nadia talked about their homes but I didn't really listen, just nodded like you have to and thought my own thoughts.

Emma, 17, 5'10", blonde hair: I like the evening, when night falls and the work of the day is done and you're free to dream, specially if you don't have exams hanging over you. For the last two years, nearly, my A Levels seemed to take all the time there was, because I wanted to do well and I'm not bright bright, like my sister Christie. She's like super-absorbent kitchen towel, she just sucks up anything, and it sticks. I think Rohini's like that probably.

On the other hand I like academic work – sometimes. The times when you sit down with an essay that's been kicking round in your head for days, all the ideas gradually growing like crystals in salt, and then you sit down in your room, quiet with the music on and just the lamp by the computer, and you write, and it comes together, sometimes well. Never never quite as well as you imagined it, but sometimes it almost does, just beyond your reach but fingertip-touching it. A sense of satisfaction and peace. The music is usually the Brandenburgs.

This evening, after all we'd done, with my skin tingling from the sun and my muscles tired from the long haul up the hill, and my headache nearly gone, I felt the grateful relief mixed with satisfaction (smugness, probably) from having done enough. Well, maybe not enough because Rohini was right, we should have found poor Fliss earlier, and then maybe she wouldn't have died. Or maybe she would anyway despite everything we did and then we'd have felt worse, probably. Anneka'd left me alone at last: good moment.

Night's the time for memories, too. When you think about what you're missing at home. I expect the rest of them were thinking that as well. I lay in the wrap I'd made for myself of clothes from the plane (good call of mine, bringing down as much as we could). Although it wasn't cold the ickles did wrap themselves up and grouped in huddles quite near the fire, and for a while I could hear some of them sobbing. 'Night, good night, sleep well,' I called to them, and some of them answered.

Then I looked up at the stars (different stars from home, Southern Hemisphere), bright against velvet black, no moon. I was looking up through a palm tree and its pointy leaves sliced the sky for me. I could have thought about all the things we had to do in the morning and made a mental list (I usually do that), and surely this if any was the time to do it. But I didn't, I just thought about Rick and saying goodbye to him, and whether he was thinking about me now. I'd said I'd ring him as soon as we got to Australia, whatever the time difference, and he said he wanted me to. So he'd know we were missing. What would he think? What would he do?

He's the kind of person who acts what he feels. If he really loved me he'd do something. But he's not self-dramatising (he's going to be a scientist of some sort, physics I think) and maybe he'd think there's nothing he could do, and he wouldn't expect the worst immediately.

Neither would my parents. They wouldn't really worry, not for long. Because they'd hear we'd been found, we were safe. Although of course not all of us were safe. Some of the competition winners were dead. Tomorrow, we should make a list of survivors. So when the rescuers came they'd know immediately and set people's minds at rest.

And meanwhile, here I was on a beautiful island in a beautiful sea, young and strong and not bad-looking, with all my life ahead of me.

Anneka, 11, 5'1", mousy hair: I woke up in the middle of the night, jump. Everyone was asleep. Some of them were snoring and breathing like dogs, that kind of gentle snuffle which I like. I had a dog (mongrel, sandy-colour, called Maxi) that Granpa gave me when I was still living with Mum but she didn't like it because she said it was another responsibility, and what she meant though she didn't say was that I was already one responsibility too many. Which is probably why I try to take responsibility for myself. Not very well.

But anyway, about Maxi, she gave him away after I hadn't taken him out and he'd made a mess in the kitchen. At least she said she gave him away. She may have had him killed because I heard her talking to one of her men friends and she said something about the dog being put down and I thought that meant like being got at, cos I get put down all the time, but I asked Granpa and he said it wasn't the same with dogs, it meant killing them. I said, I want to die when I'm put down but he told me to shut it cos the next thing I'd be doing was flashing my knickers and batting my eyes. None of which made sense to me so I gave up trying to understand. I knew Maxi'd gone.

Which is where I started, with the snuffle noises the others were making, like Maxi's snuffle in my ear when I smuggled him into bed with me, which Mum didn't like. I lay for a while listening to the snuffles and looking at the stars. It'd probably be a while before I went back to sleep. Granpa told me, if you're not sleeping don't lie there feeling sorry for yourself, do something useful. So I thought I'd have a wee and a drink of water.

It was dark dark dark and I moved very slowly, waiting till I could see, cos that takes a while. Night vision, it's called. When I got my night vision I saw that edging towards the spring I'd almost reached Alice. She was nearly at my feet. Sound asleep, sprawled, with her arms wide up behind her head. She looked like a photograph for a film. She looked amazing. Not that I'd like to look like her because her tits are quite big so she's probly mad but if you want to look female you'd want to look like her. And come to that, if you are female, you want to look female, except not if you've got my granpa. It's too muddling, I won't think about it.

I was standing near Alice and not thinking about tits when something popped into my head, and when it popped in I had a surge of guilt because I couldn't understand why I hadn't thought of it before, how could I have forgotten it, how could I have just gone to bed? Because we hadn't kept looking for the man. When it got dark, after we'd found the poor lady, Rohini said we couldn't keep looking so we didn't. But there was still an old man out there, maybe like my granpa, and he might be ill and we might be able to help him . . .

By myself? How could I by myself? I'd have to get Emma to help me. But I couldn't wake her, she'd be angry, I'd be a nuisance, and I must must must keep Emma a friend.

I went to look by myself, where Rosie'd said she'd seen him. I could see quite well by now, not colours of course just shades of grey, and I kept well on the beach because under the trees there were shadows. When I got a bit further up the beach I started hearing the noise. There was always the shush of the sea, the sea outside the reef, but it was far away so it was quiet, and the rustle and sudden noises which I didn't know what made them, in the bushes and stuff under the trees. But this noise was different, it went on steadily and it was clicky and rustly. Strange. It made me stop, that I didn't know what it was. The hairs on my back went up. I was spooked.

The noise sounded close as well. I stood still. The noise was coming from the beach ahead of me as far as I could tell. It's hard to tell, with sounds.

At first it was a blur, a darker blur on the sand. With movement in it. A big blur, covering large patches of sand. Roundabout where we'd buried the lady, maybe, though I couldn't be sure. A sort of stone-monster, a big blobby moving stone-monster, maybe a stone-monster that you only get on tiny islands right in the middle of a huge nowhere sea.

Then something clicked behind my eyes like a camera coming into focus and I could see. It wasn't one monster. It was gadzillions of small ones, little moving clicking things, going in and out of the lady's grave.

One of them scuttled towards me and I nearly screamed. I bit on my hand so as not to scream and wake everybody up, particularly Emma. It was only a crab, a crab, I told myself hopping backwards away from it, a crab like you see plastic models of in Asda by the fresh-fish counter. They were good to eat, people said they were good to eat. Tomorrow I'd tell everyone about them and we'd work out a way to catch them and cook them and eat them and Emma would be pleased . . .

I kept hopping and the crab kept coming and then, like it knew I was there, it swerved and scuttled away from the beach and into the bushes. When I didn't have to watch it any more I turned and ran, back to the fire, back to the others. The old man would be all right. Or he was probly dead. But I was certainly scared, and I'm a coward. You've gotta know your limitations.

Meet the Island

It was exciting when the plane crashed.

Up to then it had been a typical hurricane, a small one. Trees whipping and bending (not many uprooted), the sea lashing, birds taking cover, standard features. Then engine, chug chug chug, cutting out, crash bounce tear smash, engine roar, crash tear tear tear crash flames flames roar.

I had a genuine **MAJOR DISASTER**. I'd never had one of those before. I'd be featured all over the world. Body bags. TV crews. Live from – what would they call me?

I've plenty of names. Each time humans came they thought they owned me, and ownership started with naming. Eastern Island, Sunrise Island, Parrot Island, Crab Island, all in their own languages. My personal favourite was Beautiful Island.

Let's assume they'll bring the tragic story live from Beautiful Island.

I've been waiting to tell a story, any story, for 25,000 years.

So why haven't I?

Because I'm a land mass. There are advantages to

being a land mass and I'm a particularly interesting one. I'm a volcanic island, about 60,000 years old, 2 miles by 1½ miles, and currently uninhabited. I have fresh water and clean white beaches on my eastern side. I harbour a wide range of species, both plant and animal, many of which are edible by humans. My volcano is dormant: it last erupted in 1240 AD, and since I happened to be uninhabited then too, nobody was hurt, and I've been even more fertile ever since. My climate is good. I'm a Solomon Island, in the far south-east of Temotu Province. My temperature ranges between 25°C and 29°C year-round, I have moderate rainfall and humidity, specially if you avoid the monsoon season (January–April) and I've just had a hurricane, so there probably won't be another one for a while.

Should you wish to visit me – as I hope you will – you can access further details, with latitude and longitude and navigation advice, on my website, www.imarock.com. Information is updated regularly, with current weather reports. Unfortunately at the moment the only way to reach me is by sea, though if I were developing myself I'd build a heli-pad.

A disadvantage of being a land mass, however, is that you don't *do* much. Over a million years or so you might drift a little. If you're lucky enough to have a volcano, you erupt. If you're interested in natural history you can count your species and watch them evolve. But those entertainments pall. Twenty-five thousand years ago, when the first human beings landed on me, I found them enthralling.

First, hunter-gatherers from New Guinea, then

Austronesians, Lapitans, Melanesians, Polynesians. Their departures varied. Some killed each other and one tribe loaded everyone into canoes and sailed out to sea, knowing they would die. (If I had feelings, I'd have been hurt by that.) Some were eaten by visiting Tongans.

Then came the passing white man. Spanish, Portuguese, British, French, Americans, Irish, Australians, Germans. They stopped by, then went away again, because, let's face it, I'm too small. And from their point of view I had no valuable resources. No minerals, no sandalwood, and very few inhabitants to enslave.

In the Second World War the Americans and Japanese fought round me but the only souvenir left is an American bomber which crashed on the slopes of my volcano. It was completely overgrown in two years.

So, as you see, I've had plenty of experience of human beings, one way and another, and I've always liked them. Not many land masses do. Western Europe (which has theories about everything) says my interest in humans probably stems from a complex set up during my formation, but I pay no attention, because Western Europe is hundreds of millions of years old and therefore bossy and bitter. I know why I like human beings. It's because they invent things.

I spotted that 25,000 years ago. A hunter-gatherer tribe (about fifty of them) were perched on me, briefly; the first humans I knew. The leader took his brother's wife into my forest, for sex. She struggled a little, but not much, so I don't think she minded, and she backed him up when his brother found them and the leader

65

killed him and told the rest of the tribe a heavy branch fell on his head.

He described the incident in such detail, I almost believed him at first. Then I remembered I knew what had happened, and it wasn't what he'd said, and after that I started really listening to what they said and comparing it with what I knew, and a lot of the time it didn't match up.

The idea appealed to me so much that I tried it myself, but (as a beginner) not very skilfully. I told southern Italy that my volcano was bigger than its volcano. Agreed, it was foolish, but I was unprepared for Italy's reaction. I apologised profusely and eventually Italy let it drop. Only two millennia later.

I'd learnt my lesson, though. I needed another audience. I needed an audience of humans, who understood fiction. Or, to put it another way, who understood being interested in what happened to one person out of millions in one species out of millions on one planet out of millions in one galaxy out of millions. That belief is crucial for humans. In every tribe, millennium after millennium, they've designated people whose job it is to be interested. They call them gods, or holy men, or kings, or presidents, or psychiatrists, or mothers.

Then came the Net, and a chance for me to read. For ten years now I've been reading and reading. To begin with I chose **RECENT NON-FICTION**, because I wanted to find out what humans knew. The answer was, plenty. Some of it was weak on detail – they haven't a grip on volcanoes, still – and in lots of areas, like evolution and astronomy and quantum physics and neurology and genetics, they still don't know much at all, although they pretend they do. They could just write 'here be monsters' and be done with it.

Then I indulged myself and read stories. Any stories, though I must confess the ones I liked best were set on islands. I think I'm ready to try one of my own, on the Net of course, which must be where you're reading this. If I hadn't told you what I was, you wouldn't have known. I considered not telling you, but then I realised that communicating is all the fun.

So, when dawn came on the day after the crash, I looked for my cast of characters. It was most disappointing: they were all female. And many of them were young, too young to count as people.

Even land masses know that females don't do things, much. They bear children and gather food and cook and clean and gossip and adorn themselves, and if they're lucky they provoke a sexual contest between the males, the real people. They are never priests or soldiers or medicine men. They never invent. They just struggle for survival, then die, and if they're very lucky they're remembered as 'the mother of' or 'the wife of'. My cast contained no men: therefore, no conflict. Unless they fought for the title Most Beautiful or Chieftainess of the Cooking-pots, and even then, without men to watch them, would they care?

Not expecting much, I went back to the Net and researched. And found that modern thinking had changed completely. (I'd've picked it up before if I hadn't ignored **GENDER ISSUES**, because they sounded so boring.) Now, apparently, everyone knew that females are *more* interesting than males: stronger, nicer, kinder, more peaceable, more nurturing (they'd always been nurturing but now nurturing was a good thing to be, not just necessary-but-dull), and they should rule the world. Or at least the western females knew that. Perhaps I had a good cast after all. Better still, these particular females were minor celebrities (they kept talking about their websites).

If modern female thinking was correct, the situation was ideal. With no men to contaminate them, they'd build an ideal society, for the short (I hoped not too short) time they stayed on me.

I had an initial problem in telling them apart. The older ones were comparatively easy: the little ones functioned as a pack. I concentrated. Eventually I identified them by hair colour, height and age. Then I waited eagerly for Paradise to unfold.

CHAPTER FIVE

Rohini, 17, 5'2", black hair: I wake up first, just before the sun comes up, with faint light bleeding into the sky where it meets the sea. Enough light to see by.

I wake angry. I'd been incompetent and ineffective. My ideas are OK, my execution of them'd been rubbish. Lucky I've woken. I can get masses done on my own before the endless cat's-cradle of appeasement starts: don't mean to criticise, oh just a suggestion, no of course you're right to sit on your tight little buns and paint your face while Rome burns.

All the rest of them are still asleep. I pee and water myself then head up to the other end of the beach. Objective 1: go through Fliss the Flustered's bag to find a list of competition winners, check the living, enable roll-calls. Objective 2: sort through the plundered suitcases for useful material.

Slight delay to objective 1 because I have to detour and rebury what's left of Fliss-the-by-now-scavenged (first thought, vultures; second thought, happened at night, most likely crabs). Hygienic creatures, really. I'd've left her un-reburied if it wasn't for the inevitable aftermath, chorus of yuks and eeuws followed by extensive mutual indulgence, restorative bun-sitting and face-painting.

After that I wash my hands in the lagoon water and think about Granma Sitaram, and what she'd've said about me burying a half-eaten body with my bare hands. Remember your caste, remember your caste. But there are no castes, not any more, and I'm not a Hindu any more. I don't exactly know what I am, but it isn't that. Not even a tiny bit. My caste's an intellectual one, though I can't say that out loud. What I am is a child of the Enlightenment. Except that the Enlightenment's intellectually out of date, now, and I'm really not post-modern. Post-modern's a lot like being Hindu. Syncretic. Bits everywhere. I like things linear, and clean.

It takes a little while to find her bag, but when I get it, there indeed is a list. Originally there'd been thirty of us. Now I guess it's about twenty-one. A high proportion. Check who we've got, task for later.

Next, the suitcases. What a mess. What a mess. They haven't just opened them, they've plundered them, like looters in riots, and scattered the contents everywhere, some of them at the water's edge so they're soaked and smelling. And mixed in among it, the clothes that the kids had taken off, the competition clothes, which they'd just dropped and left. They'll want them, of course. Unless they want to spend all their time here (which could, worst scenario, be a long time, since rescuers haven't come yet – why?) wearing the stupid gear they'd picked yesterday.

There's some new stuff as well. I suppose it's new: it's unopened. Most likely disgorged from another section of the aircraft's hold.

I set to work sorting. Competition clothes first. Men's clothes, women's clothes, kids' and babies' stuff, toilet articles, food (mostly tins of biscuits, etc.) books and magazines, guides, footwear, underwear (we'd especially be needing that), presents, duty-free alcohol, cigarettes, stationery, mobile phones, teddy-bears, laptops, clocks, CDs, radios, Walkmans, mosquito spirals, sunblock, kettle, tea-making equipment, lots and lots of pills – aspirin, heart pills – and what jewellery was left after the barbarians had barbarianed-up.

Oh, the heavy weight of things. Melancholy, when the owners are gone. Just valueless clutter. Powerful reminders of how fragile life is, and how futile our efforts and hopes are.

I make myself push it away. Now isn't the time for feeling. Now's the time for thinking. Not that thinking, at this moment, is very appealing. I feel a strong tug, almost physical, of fear. Yes, it is quite physical, right in my guts. It might be just the beginning of the runs from the breadfruit, coconut and bananas.

I keep sorting the things. Lot of useful stuff. Alcohol: worrying. I can just imagine the problem if the kids start drinking it. I consider pouring it all away. Some of it's broken anyway. No, it'd take too long, and I don't know how long I've got before the others wake up and start snatching things they want out of the piles.

After the sorting, that patch of the beach looks more respectable for when the rescuers come. Which they must. I have to keep believing they will, and planning as if they won't, and above all not imagine too much. Imagination is the enemy within.

Anneka, 11, 5'1", mousy hair: Nobody had woken up yet as far as I could see and Emma was still sleeping. I got up and walked along the beach. Slowly, so I'd see the crabs in good time. The dawn light was pink like in a film but I could see quite well. No sign of the crabs. Good. Cept maybe not good, because if I could see them I'd know to keep away from them. If I couldn't see them they must have hidden somewhere and maybe they'd come out at me, suddenly.

My mind was giving me a picture of them, all together, a great crawling pile, like one animal with lots of bits. I tried to keep the picture out but it kept coming back and I stopped walking in case I put my feet on top of where they were hidden, underneath.

That was stupid, I told myself. That was really stupid. There'd been gadzillions of them, they couldn't all be under the sand in one place.

I still didn't want to move, though. The crab-picture kept coming back. I made myself look ahead, further down the beach, right to the suitcases. There was someone there. Rohini. Just knowing she was there made the picture go away and I got moving again.

Now I was going past the heaps of seaweed and stuff with dead birds and fish in them that were beginning to rot yesterday. Something was different about them. Today they smelled of seaweed and not much else. The crabs must have worked on them too, so aksherly (I told myself) the crabs were very useful. Pity they have to be ugly and scary too.

I kept myself going along, walking much nearer the sea so not to notice the grave as I got near it cos I didn't want to see the body. Cept when I got near, it was buried again. Rohini must have done it. A scary, messy job. Now she was sorting all the things from the suitcases into piles, and she didn't look that pleased to see me.

D'you think they'll come today, I said.

They'll come, she said, with that empty, reassuring voice that grown-ups use when they aren't listening to what they're saying, and they aren't talking to you but to themselves as if there was an audience for how well they're dealing with kids. Then she turned her back on me and kept working.

I could tell she didn't want me there.

I wanted Emma to wake. I wanted Emma. Maybe I should go back and see her. But it was a long walk back, and hard in the sand. Maybe I'd spend the rest of my life with my feet sticking in the sand and me pulling them up, walking up and down and up and down in the glare of the sun which was much less of a kind sun than the sun at home. It was cruel, like the skulls with holes for eyes; it didn't care for us. I felt homesick and I wanted my granpa.

I hate it when people want me to go away, so I usually do, quickly, but there was something I had to try. Should we look for the man? I said.

Not just the two of us, said Rohini. Maybe when the others wake up . . .

If they'll help, I said.

She looked at me, this time as if I was real. We'll work something out, don't worry, she said.

I didn't believe her. Do you think there is a man? I asked her. I mean a live man, or d'you think the crabs have made a skull of him?

I don't know, she said, nearly cross. I think she felt guilty. I thought she had the night before. Guilty makes people act odd. Maybe cos she was guilty she wouldn't search, and I didn't know how to make her. I can't wait to be grown up and then I can get what I want without having to deal with people all the time, try and persuade them. When I'm grown up I can just say what I want and take it, instead of trying to please, which I'm not actually very good at. I never please my mother and I often don't please my granpa. But when he tells me off I know he loves me too, he must. Mum says I don't know why he bothers with you, he never did with me. I think he bothers with me from love. What'll happen when I grow tits, I've asked him again and again, but he never answers proply, he just says that's a good question, which of all the stupid things grown-ups say is nearly the stupidest.

Anyway what with all of it, Mum and Grandpa, I'm awkward. I always do the wrong thing.

But one thing I've found is nearly always the right thing is to go away, so I'm not a nuisance. So I started to go away, back to Emma.

I'd hardly moved before Rohini said, D'you want something to do?

I jumped at it. I like to be useful. So she gave me a list and a pencil and told me what she wanted.

74

Emma, 17, 5'10", blonde hair: Once more, although I was awake, I kept trying to sleep. No headache this time, so I felt better, but the great weight of where we were and what we had to do was heavier, if anything. I didn't want to get up and face it.

The sun was hot on my face already. How late was it? How strong was the sun going to get?

It was Anneka again, shaking me. 'Wake up, Emma. Please wake up.' She was crying. Oh, god, she'd managed to upset herself before breakfast. Not that it would be a breakfasty breakfast. I couldn't face cold breadfruit but I'd have to eat something; we all would.

I could hear a background of murmuring complaint as regular as the heave of the sea.

'I'm burnt . . .'

'I feel sick . . .'

'I wanna go home . . .'

Sob sob sob . . .

'Cannave Cocopops . . .'

'Where's my clean pants . . .'

And specifically, in my ear, 'Wake up, Emma, please wake up.'

'What is it?' I grumped, opening one eye and immediately shutting it again, against the flood of sun.

'Rohini gave me a job to do.'

'And?'

'And they wouldn't let me do it. Look, see, she gave me the list of all of us that there were originally and she wanted me to find out how many were missing, only not to upset them by letting them know how many were missing, not that I think they'd really care but just pretend to, so she said just ask them what

75

their names are, the ones we're not sure of, the kids. We know the older ones, but we need to sort out the kids. So I started asking them what their names are, and the first one was Rosie and I knew her and then the pony one told me her name was Susan, but the third one was Tamsin and she just said Britney Spears, and the others started to laugh and then they all said Britney Spears.'

She showed me her list. She'd written Britney Spears eight times. It was early and I'm slow in the morning, so I laughed. Later in the day I wouldn't have, however silly it looked. Which, of course, it did.

She walked away without pausing or looking back, and then I felt guilty, of course, and then I felt annoyed with her, of course.

'Emma! Emma!' It was Vanessa. Pink, overheated, puffing. She should either lose weight and exercise or stop running, I thought crossly. 'There's a row. Come quickly. It's dreadful. Rohini and Alice. It's awful. Very, very horrible. Come, quickly.'

From the Island

The row looks promising. All drama is conflict, it says on the Net. So perhaps what we have here is not prose fiction, but a play.

CHAPTER SIX

The Meeting on the Second Day

(only a working title)

First performed in the Clearing, Beautiful Island, Temotu Province, Solomon Islands, with the following cast. All characters portrayed by Themselves.

Alice, 18
Emma, 17
Rohini, 17
Deborah (Debs), 16
Rouchelle, 16
Tawheeda, 16

The Goody-goods

Vanessa, 15
Charlotte, 15
Mei Lin, 15

Nadia, 14

The Ickles

Tamsin, 12
Anneka, 11

Susan, 11 (Pony ickle, heard baby)
Rosie, 11 (claims she saw man)
Eight so-far-unnamed Ickles (also known as Britney
  Spears)

Plus

The Baby

The Can't Bird

Present in spirit, voice only

Tamsin's mum

Directed by: Themselves
Designed by: Evolution
Lighting by: The Sun

Scene One

Morning, two hours after sunrise. The Clearing. An outstanding area of natural beauty. Limpid water cascades through luxuriant foliage to debouch in a sparkling rock-pool set amid pure white sand. Three fallen tree-trunks in a semi-circle facing the pool. A phalanx of parrots, ornamentally distributed in the branches of lofty trees, follow the proceedings with their intelligent, questing eyes, occasionally ruffling and preening their richly tinted plumage. Largely unseen, over three million insects ply their trade beneath the loamy leaves heaped around.

ROHINI *stands, foursquare, centre.* ALICE *is berating her.*

ALICE: *(furious)* Some cheek, some cheek you've got. Where d'you get off telling me what I can and can't have?

ROHINI: *(reasonable)* I didn't tell *you* anything. I just pointed out to Vanessa that I'd sorted out the suitcases and I didn't want anyone taking anything till we'd had a meeting –

ALICE: *(with profound contempt)* Meeting!

ROHINI: – a meeting to sort out who has what, so it's fair –

ALICE: Fair!

ROHINI: I didn't know she wanted the eye-makeup remover for *you* –

ALICE: Didn't know!

ROHINI: – though now I look at you I can see, it has blotched and streaked a bit, hasn't it?

ALICE: *(viciously)* You think you're so clever.

ROHINI: And I am. Very clever. Whereas you think you're wonderful, and you're perfectly common-place –

ALICE: Common!

ROHINI: – with the conversational resources of a parrot. You're vain, spoilt, selfish and stupid. With quite good looks that won't last long. Poor you. And now I'm calling a meeting so that *all* of us can survive, and be safe, and be comfortable.

ALICE: *(viciously)* Sod you, then.

VANESSA: *(off)* Oh, stop them, please stop them.

ROUCHELLE: *(off)* Whass goin on?

NADIA: *(off)* It's the rumble in the jungle.

ROHINI *sounds the rape alarm. Two prolonged bursts.* THE BABY *wails, (off). The girls start to enter the clearing.* ALICE *stops spluttering and sits in the middle of the centre log, arms folded, scowling.* DEBS, *rocking and patting* THE BABY, *sits beside her.*

ROHINI: *(ignoring* ALICE*'s obvious sulk)* Can you all sit down, please?

The other girls sit down, older girls in the middle, ICKLES *towards the sides, pushing, shoving and squabbling. General noise. Some of the girls pick up the hostility radiating from* ALICE *and cast sidelong glances at her.*

ROHINI: Shush, hush, all right everyone. There's things you need to know. We've all got to work together, look after each other and share, and if we do, then it'll be better for all of us. Safer, more comfortable, happier and fairer.

81

The noise level subsides. ALICE *scowls, squirms in her seat, makes* ROUCHELLE *swap places with her so* ALICE *is now the other side of* DEBS.

ROHINI: We're going to be rescued soon, for sure, and then we'll be going home to our families. When we do that, we all want to be healthy. So we've got to protect our skin with sunblock –

ALICE *laughs, whispers to* DEBS, *who laughs too. They both stare at* ROHINI *contemptuously. The others look at them and some of* THE ICKLES *begin to whisper.*

ROHINI: – and eat properly, and drink clean water –

ALICE: *(impatiently)* The water *is* clean.

ROHINI: Not if we pee upstream. Or wash in the pool. Or don't dispose of our tampons properly.

ALICE: *(disgusted)* Puh-leeze! Do you mind?

ROHINI: We should bury them or put them on the fire. Not throw them in the pool, where I just found one.

A chorus of retching noises from THE ICKLES.

THE ICKLES: I never . . . yes you did, I saw you . . . twasn't me . . . yes twas . . . megayuk and upchuck . . .

ROHINI: And we can't wash Baby's nappies out in the pool, either.

DEBS: *(viciously)* What's with this *we*, Paki? You want to call me, call me by name, I've got a name, it's Deborah, and I'm the one's had the baby all night.

BABY *cries.*

ALICE: *(smirking, then serious-faced)* Hey, you upset the baby.

ROHINI: That's absurd.

BABY *wails.*

DEBS: Baby's really upset. You hurt his feelings.

THE ICKLES: *(some clustering round* THE BABY*)* Ahhh . . . poor baby . . . there there . . . sweet . . .

ROHINI: *(impatiently)* That's completely ridiculous.

ALICE: Ridiculous? What'you saying, his feelings are ridiculous?

THE BABY *continues wailing.* DEBS *makes no attempt to quiet him, smirking.* THE ICKLES *ooh and aah.*

DEBS: I gorra wash the nappies somewhere.

ROHINI: *(taking a deep breath, controlling herself)* We'll talk about that later, OK? The main thing is, remember to keep the pool clean.

THE CAN'T BIRD: Caaan't, caaan't . . .

THE ICKLES: It's him, it's the man . . . I wish he'd stop, he should stop . . . make him stop . . .

ROHINI: That's only a bird, it's a bird. It just sounds like a person.

THE CAN'T BIRD: Caaan't, caaan't . . .

THE ICKLES: Make it stop . . . I hate it . . . I'm scared . . .

ROHINI: It's only a bird. Forget it.

TAMSIN: Who're you, giving orders?

ROHINI: Shush, shush . . . *(Noise level rises.)* I'll give you all a pencil and a piece of paper, and . . . *(noise level rises further, she is inaudible.)*

NADIA: *(getting up, standing beside* ROHINI, *shouts)* Shurrup! Orright! Shurrup! Sit down!

TAMSIN: Why?

NADIA: *(facing her down, jocular)* Cos I'll smash your face in if you don't, orright?

THE GOODY-GOODS: That's a bit . . . hold on . . . hang on a minute . . .

TAMSIN'S MUM: That's violating our rights.

NADIA: I'll violate your face in a minute.

TAMSIN'S MUM: That's actionable.

NADIA: More like painful. Shurrup. *(Pacing up and down in front of the protesting* ICKLES, *threateningly.)* C'mon, Emma, gissa hand here.

EMMA: *(reluctant, doesn't move)* I don't quite . . .

ROUCHELLE: *(joins* NADIA, *takes the other end of the logs, paces threateningly)* Shut it, you lot. I said shut it. We've gorra get sorted, right? Right? Shut it.

NADIA: *(aside to* ROUCHELLE*)* Thanks, Kilburn.

ROUCHELLE: *(aside to* NADIA*)* My pleasure, Eltham.

Silence.

ALICE: *(imitably)* Hell-o. Puh-leeze. This isn't getting us anywhere.

ROHINI: Back to London, surely.

ALICE: *(furiously)* What?

THE CAN'T BIRD: Caaan't . . .

NADIA: SHURRUP BIRD!

THE ICKLES *laugh.*

NADIA: *(firmly)* OK, Rohini. You want these pencils and paper given out?

ROHINI: Yes.

NADIA *and* ROUCHELLE *distribute pencils and paper.* DEBS *waves them away.* NADIA *wedges the paper between* DEBS *and* THE BABY, *and the pencil in* DEBS' *fingers.*

VANESSA: *(raises her hand)* Rohini?

ROHINI: Yes?

THE GOODY-GOODS: The fire's gone out, it went out overnight, and we've dried lots of wood to start it again, put wood out on the beach in the sun and it's drying, only we don't have a lighter, we can't light it, we dont' have a lighter.

NADIA: You had mine.

THE GOODY-GOODS: *(exchanging glances)* Well, we did, yes we did, but we . . . well it . . . we don't have it now . . . no, we don't have it now . . .

DEBS: I took it, orright?

THE GOODY-GOODS: It's nice having a fire, we need a fire, it's good to have the smoke, like if they're looking for us on satellite pictures and there's smoke, they'll notice the smoke, if the island's uninhabited then there's smoke, they'll know it's us, can we have it back please?

DEBS: Nah. It's history. I chucked it.

ALICE: *(flatly)* I needed to see. To do my make-up. The sun was going down.

ROUCHELLE: *(sarcastically)* Brilliant. Really brilliant.

THE ICKLES: I couldn't see either . . . I could . . . that was before . . . I never got to paint my face, all the red had gone . . .

ROHINI: Never mind, I've found more lighters, I'll give you one after the meeting, OK? There's lots of things we need to arrange quickly and we can't do it if we all talk at once, so just listen for a bit, please.

THE ICKLES: We are listening . . . get on with it . . . that's not fair . . . cannava different pencil . . . she's got a pen, I wanna pen . . . 'snot a pen, it just looks like a pen . . . cannava pencil that looks like a pen . . .

TAMSIN: Why do we haveta listen to you?

NADIA: Because she's got something to say, orright?

TAMSIN: When're they gonna rescue us? What about the mobiles?

THE ICKLES: *(delighted, relieved)* Yeah . . . that's what we gorra do . . . call home on the mobiles . . . call home . . . call home . . . the mobiles . . . yeah, the mobiles.

ROHINI: The mobiles don't work. I've tried them. None of them are powerful enough. You need a special sort –

THE ICKLES: *(overriding her)* Why did *you* try them . . .

that's not fair, I wanna try . . . they must work, they must, they must, they always do . . .

TAMSIN: So whenna we gonna be RESCUED? Why don't you TELL US? What're you HIDING?

ROHINI: I'm not hiding anything. We'll be rescued soon, I hope. We all hope, soon. But we've got to organise ourselves just in case they take a while to find us.

PONY ICKLE: *(whinnies and paws the sand)* Why don't the grown-ups sort it out?

ROHINI: There are no grown-ups. Alice and Emma and me, we're the closest you've got.

NADIA: If you lot don't shut it, you'll be grown-ups by the time we get to the point.

THE BABY *wails.* ALICE *squirms, scowls, gets up, sits down in the place vacated by* ROUCHELLE.

ROHINI: So this is what we need to do. Just imagine they don't rescue us for a bit. We've only got a limited supply of clothes and things from the suit-cases. We each need our own proper clothes, the competition clothes, and a spare pair of pants, and sunblock, and –

THE ICKLES: My sweatshirt's got blood all over . . . I want factor thirty, my mum says I've gorra have factor thirty . . . that gear's rank, I'm not wearing that stuff . . . I lost my trainers, I got no trainers . . .

THE BABY *wails.* DEBS *is not genuinely trying to quiet it, first with water, then with rocking.*

ROHINI: And I've found the summer competition clothes they were going to give us, so there's enough new for everyone, shorts and T-shirts.

ONE ICKLE: I need a training bra, 've you gorra training bra?

OTHER ICKLES: What you gonna train? You got nothing to train!

TAMSIN: Pip-tits! Pip-tits!

BRA ICKLE: *sobs.* BABY *wails.*

OTHER ICKLES: Pip-tits! Pip-tits!

NADIA: *(to* TAMSIN*)* Pip-tits yourself. Shurrup! (*To the other* ICKLES.*)* Shurrup!

ROHINI: We need to allocate resources.

NADIA: *(aside to* ROHINI*)* Don't tell em *why*, tell em *what to do*. Keep it simple.

ROHINI: OK. First, write your name on the piece of paper I've given you. Then write which of the chores you'll do. Like collecting food, cooking, tidying, keeping the fire, maybe building shelters, helping to search the island, looking after the baby . . .

ALICE: *(flatly)* Debs has the baby. I said so yesterday. She can look after it. The baby's with Debs.

ROHINI: Why? It's really hard work. We should share it.

EMMA: We should share it.

ALICE: She knows about babies. She's a woman of

courage. Like on her website, it says. She's a woman of courage.

BABY *wails.*

DEBS: I . . .

TAMSIN: Alice said. Last night. Alice said. I heard her.

THE ICKLES: So did I . . . me too . . . me too . . . Alice said . . .

DEBS *makes to speak:* ALICE *quells her with a savage glance.*

ALICE: *(triumphantly)* That's sorted then.

TAMSIN: When you gonna tell us about food? I want some proper food. Frubs. Nutty Corners.

NADIA: Keep writing. Put your hand up when you've finished, we'll take them in.

TAMSIN: This is just like school. It was sposed to be a treat . . . We're victims . . . We want counselling to get over the traw-mar . . .

THE ICKLES: Counselling, yeah . . . to get over the traw-mar . . . What's traw-mar? . . . It's what you need counselling for, Pip-tits . . .

VANESSA: *(raises her hand)* If we'll do anything to help, is it OK to put 'anything', or should we still make the list?

ROHINI: Just put 'anything', that's fine. Thanks.

ALICE *writes her name, then stares blankly at her piece of paper.* VANESSA *raises her hand.*

THE GOODY-GOODS: We've been wondering, you

know what we wrote our competition thing on, our survey and essay that won, it was on PMS, pre-menstrual syndrome, and our findings were start-ling, well they startled us, well they didn't startle me that's why I suggested it, well they startled Mei Lin and me, they didn't startle me, I *know* that Charlotte . . .

ROHINI: Vanessa and Mei Lin were startled. Charlotte was less startled. Fine. What's your point?

THE GOODY-GOODS: Our findings, our findings are the point, we found that PMS makes a *real differ-ence* to how girls behave, women we mean, how women behave, mood swings, rattiness, inability to concentrate, can't cope, burst into tears, behave irra-tionally, feeling of tiredness, can't cope with school-work . . .

THE ICKLES, *bored, start a general mumbling. One makes a paper aeroplane.*

NADIA: Shurrup! Where you going here, Vanessa?

THE GOODY-GOODS: Not just Vanessa, no it's all three of us, it's them as well, what we mean, it makes a difference so we could write on our pieces of paper when our periods are due, then everyone would make allowances, we could all be sensitive to each other's needs . . .

BRA ICKLE: I don't have my period yet.

OTHER ICKLES: *(mocking laughter, pointing)* Bay-bee, bay-bee, bay-bee.

ALICE: *(roused to interest)* How come you entered the

competition, then? We had to say what tampon we use.

BRA ICKLE: Mummy lied.

ALICE: *(satisfied)* Oh, right.

ROHINI: OK, if you want to, put the date of the first day of your period on your piece of paper as well. When we've collected all the papers we're going along the beach to the suitcases and you can all get your competition clothes and a spare pair of pants and mark them, so they don't get mixed up. I've got some permanent markers. And you need sunblock, and there's plenty of that, but we've got to share. And we shouldn't take anything we don't actually need, because it doesn't belong to us.

TAMSIN: How do you know? It might.

ROHINI: If anyone finds their own bag, it's theirs of course, to do what they like with.

DEBS: *(sarcastic)* Thanks a bunch.

THE GOODY-GOODS: *(raising their hands)* Rohini . . . Rohini . . . Rohini . . .

ROHINI: Yes?

THE GOODY-GOODS: We've got a problem. Did you find any surgical spirit, cos Charlotte's piercing, her bellybutton, I had it done specially for Australia, you shouldn't have, your mother won't like it, she won't mind, why didn't you tell her then, anyway it's going manky, no it isn't, you said it was, we need surgical spirit, did you find any?

91

ROHINI: I'll have a look. Then when we've sorted out the things we'll work out who's going to do what . . .

PONY ICKLE: *(sobbing)* Why haven't they come for us? Why haven't they come? They should have come.

ALICE *is still staring at her piece of paper.* DEBS *whispers something to her. They discuss, in whispers.* ALICE *writes.*

ROHINI: *(reassuringly)* They'll come soon, of course they will. And meanwhile, we're very lucky.

THE ICKLES: LUCKY? My bites are sore . . . I got bruises ALL OVER . . . I wanna go HOME . . . I want my MUM . . . waaah . . .

ROHINI: We're *very* lucky. We're alive, and the other people who were on the plane aren't. Including some of the other competition winners.

PONY ICKLE: *(sobbing)* Megan . . . Megan . . . she just went in the sea . . .

ROHINI: I'm really sorry, er –

NADIA: *(checking piece of paper)* Susan. Her name is Susan.

ROHINI: Was Megan a friend of yours, Susan?

PONY ICKLE: *(sobbing)* My *best* friend . . .

THE GOODY-GOODS: Poor you . . . that's awful . . . we're so sorry . . .

ALICE: That's awful, poor you, poor, poor you. We're all really, really sorry, aren't we guys?

NEARLY ALL: We're so sorry . . . really sorry . . . really, really sorry . . .

ROHINI: So as I was saying, we're the lucky ones. And we're on a beautiful island, it's warm, we've got water and plenty of food . . .

TAMSIN: Breadfruit, yuk!

THE ICKLES: Spiders, yuk! . . . I've bites all over . . . I want my mum . . .

DEBS: *(loudly)* Shut it, you lot. Alice wants to tell you something.

ALICE: *(getting up, walking to centre of clearing, standing in front of Rohini)* Guys, what we've gotta do, we've gotta hold a memorial service. For our friends. And for poor Fliss. And all the poor people who died on the plane.

ROHINI: *(Taken aback)* Later, maybe . . .

ALICE: Now. We need to hold a memorial service now.

THE ICKLES: Aah . . . aah . . . yeah . . . we'll get flowers . . .

DEBS *goes to* ALICE, *whispers.*

ALICE: Yeah, well, we need time to set it up. I'll sort it out, yeah?

CHAPTER SEVEN

Anneka, 11, 5'1", mousy hair: After the meeting, I felt much better. We all knew what we were doing. Rohini was in charge. Emma had kept quiet all through, I spect because it was going all right and she isn't a show-off. I hadn't tried to sit next to her, not to be annoying.

Even the sorting of the clothes went more or less OK, though the kids fussed and squabbled and complained, but not as if they meant it, and they ended up doing what they were told.

Well, mostly they did what they were told, cept about the phones. Tho Rohini *said* not to, they stole the mobiles and they ran around with them and tried to make calls and of course it didn't work, and some of them kept dialling the numbers and crying, and that made it worse for them. They kept the mobiles anyway and started pretending to talk to each other on them and if they stood close enough of course they could hear, so it was as if they were talking on the mobiles, which seemed to make them feel better. Sometimes I just don't get being a kid. Maybe some of the others don't either, and just pretend to enjoy the STUPID things they do. Maybe I should have taken a mobile too and pretended to talk on it, just to fit in, except probly no one would have pretended to talk to me.

Most of them liked the competition summer clothes, I think. I did, and Alice must've, she took three sets. I washed myself and changed, and Nadia was making more leaf-hats and she made another for me. Then I kept close to the goody-goo – 'snot fair, calling them that – mean the three friends, and helped them.

First we collected more coconuts and ripe bananas (I'm OK with climbing trees so I went up high, mostly, with Mei Lin who also doesn't mind heights). Then we all (except Alice and Debs who were still jabbering on about a memorial service, and Emma who'd gone somewhere else) searched inwards from the beach around where Rosie said she'd seen the man. Rohini said we should pick up anything we found which might be useful or might have come since the crash. I didn't find anything but one of them did, and gave it to Rohini after. I don't know what it was.

I hadn't wanted to do the search, acksherly, cos of the crabs. Of course I didn't say, because I really wanted the search to be done, and it wouldn't have been fair not to do my share. For the search we all spaced out, Rohini told us to, which made sense, but it meant I was by myself with a bit of the jungle, going inwards from the beach. I kept thinking I'd step on the crabs, who had to be hiding somewhere, they had to be. Didn't find them though. Didn't find the man either, so maybe Rosie'd been making it up.

After the search Emma came back. She'd swum out to the part of the plane that was on the reef to look for stuff for the baby, and she'd got lots of those little pots of baby food. Also packets of snacky things they'd given us on the plane, nuts and cheesy bits. Most of the kids had one but there weren't enough to go round and of course Alice wanted two for herself and Debs. All the rest of the older ones said never mind don't bother let the ickles have them, but not Alice. I don't know zackly why we all do what Alice wants, but we do.

Around noon (Rohini said it was noon, I'm not sure how she knew) Emma said we should get out of the sun and Rohini gave out some magazines she'd found, one between two or three. I didn't get one and I wasn't in a group.

I'm never in a group. Granpa says it's because I'm too thin-skinned, I can't cope with teasing. He also says the teasing would be more friendly if I had mates. They'd still tease me but it would be mate-teasing.

Fine if you know how to get mates and stop yourself being a spare part, which I don't. It's as if I have a huge sign on my head, on the part of your own head that you can never see, blinking on and off, VICTIM VICTIM. It's partly I spose cos I'm not interested in what they're interested in.

So there I was standing alone in the sun. Emma was with Rohini, up by the baggage. They were talking. No chance there. I'd be butting in.

The only other one by herself was Susan. She'd gone the other way, quite far down towards the clearing. She was sitting in the shade, scooping the sand up with her hands and pouring it over her legs. It looked a fun thing to do.

I walked down to her and stood a bit away, not to push, and said, That looks fun.

She looked up. She was crying. Not red-faced blubbing, just sort of leaking from her eyes.

Oh, hi, she said. Not 'sif she wanted me to go away, tho to be honest not 'sif she was glad to see me either. More 'sif the whole thing was too much for her. And she didn't stop crying, but I thought, don't seem to notice it, she might be embarrassed, and Granpa says sympathy makes you soft. I don't think I agree with that zackly but I do know if you sympathise with crying people they often cry more.

I sat down beside her, kicked off my trainers and burrowed my legs into the sand like her. The top of the sand was very warm but under it was cooler, and as I scooped and poured, I liked its rough feel. I've never been to the seaside before, I said.

I live near the sea, two miles, Silver likes the beaches, she said.

Who's Silver?

Silver's my pony. It's good for horse's legs to exercise in the sea. Not the deep bit, just going along the sand in the shallow bit, the seawater's good for their legs.

How old is he?

Seven. That's a very good age for a pony. Old enough to be sensible but young enough to be strong.

How big is he?

Thirteen-three.

97

That made no sense at all. How big is that, I said.

You're not a pony person, she said. Almost wailed, actually. Which narked me. She was enough of a pony person for both of us, I reckoned. You could have too many whinnies and clops.

No, I'm not, so I need telling, I said. Tell me.

They measure horses by hands, he's thirteen hands and three inches, she said.

Whose hands? I said.

She thought, wrinkling up her forehead. She'd stopped crying. I don't know whose hand it was in the beginning, I've never asked, but it means four inches, she said.

How many centimetres is that? I said.

Just over ten, she said.

We both held our hands up and looked at them. They were easily ten centimetres. Must've been a child, I said.

Can't have been, she said. It's never children, things like that, they must be measuring crossways.

I drew a line in the sand and started measuring, using my hand longways. When I got to thirteen and a bit I drew another line. Which part of the pony is this, I said, the top of his head?

She sort of scrabbled up beside me to look. No, that's the bit at the bottom of his neck, the withers, she said, just in front of where the saddle goes, then his neck and head will be above that, see. She drew it in the sand. And he has a lovely long mane 'swell, she said. Then she drew that.

What colour is he?

Called Silver, what d'you think, silly.

White?

You say grey for horses, never white.

Why?

Because.

OK.

She kept drawing the pony in the sand, working downwards. A middle bit. Legs. It looked quite good, I thought. A bit square round the bum but then maybe it was square round the bum.

Her eyes were still leaking and by now I reckoned I could ask her. You crying about your friend?

She sat back on her heels. She didn't say anything.

Sorry, I said quickly, Sorry, didn't mean to . . .

I'm sad about Megan, she said.

Of course you are –

But I'm not crying.

OK.

It's my contact lenses. They're day ones, I change them every day. I haven't changed these. And I think I've got sand in them or something.

Oh. You could take them out?

These are all I've got. I lost the others in the crash. I can't see much without them. I'm not blind or anything –

Of course not.

– but I can't see much. I don't like it . . . I get teased . . . My first school, I'd specs, really thick ones, and they teased me. Then I got contacts and at my next school they didn't know. Megan knew. She helped me.

I'll help you, I said. I was careful not to sound too keen (saddo sucks up to saddo). But I do think you ought to take the contacts out. It could hurt your eyes.

My eyes are crap, she said.

Alice, 18, 5'8", mid-brown hair with red highlights: Most things on this sodding island are well out of order. The mobiles don't even work. And I'm worried about my muscle tone. No fitness centre here, that's for sure, no Pilates. How'm I going to maintain the assets?

Time for some kip in the shade before the service. Debs wanted to kip in the clearing with me but she's got responsibilities and the baby was keeping me awake.

My best bit so far was the party yesterday, stamping and chanting. Alice the Barbarian Queen, yeah, that's what Nadia said and that was what it was like. Haven't tried diamante body jewellery before, but now I know, I will again. Defo.

And I like being in charge. Always have been, always will be. My girl can be anything she wants to be, that's what Dads says. And I know it's true. True true true. Because I look good. And because I know what I want. Know what you want and go for it, that's what Dads says, and the race is to the strong, and I'm strong. All through. So I must've been right when I said Debs should have the baby. No matter what the rest of them say, that's what I'm going to do. So there.

Wonderful winner: Nadia, 14
From: Eltham, London, UK
Hair: Red
Eyes: Blue
Sibs: Samantha, 11
Fave celebs: Lucian Freud
Winning entry: A painting: *Girls,
            playing*
Cares about: Art
Uses: right on! **(lubricated tampon for light to
medium flow)**

This's gotta be the most beautiful place I've ever been. The most beautiful place in the world. Could be.

There's more to see than I'll ever have time for. Nearly all this morning's time was swallowed whole by what Mum calls 'taking care and taking part', when I wanted to look. I can't look while I'm taking care, not really. I want to get back up and look inside the skull place Anneka fell into, that'd be good to draw.

But I've got no paints. I need paints for the colours, just the parrots for a start. Blazing red, clear, clear yellow, zingy green, all different beaks. And the butterflies, and crabs, and fish in the lagoon, coral fish I think, *so* bright. And the peculiar plants with spiky leaves, huge across, and the mountains and mountains of puff-clouds. All this, and no paints. Rohini gave me lots of paper and pencils, so I can draw, but I need paints.

I really want to draw Alice in her Barbarian Queen gear. I looked and looked, so I'd remember, and I'm doing sketches from memory, but it's not right. I get the shape but I miss the tingle.

Emma, 17, 5'10", blonde hair: During the rest-time, when the sun was hottest, Rohini and I sat near the baggage. She said she wanted to keep an eye on it. I didn't comment on the obvious, that she couldn't watch it for ever, and that whether it was watched or not Alice would take exactly what she wanted. She'd already taken a camcorder, two cameras, and various items of clothes and jewellery. For the memorial service, no doubt.

For the moment, though, the baggage was Alice-free. She and Debs (plus baby) had gone down to the clearing. It was good to be without her.

We were making leaf-hats. It was something to do. And useful.

'Like an American film,' said Rohini.

I raised an eyebrow at her.

'The women, working together. An occasion for solidarity, and confidences, and easy tragedy.'

'How can tragedy be easy?'

'Painless, good-looking deaths, and the sorrow goes when you leave the cinema.'

My current hat wasn't working. I tucked the ruined leaves into the foliage behind me and began another.

'Nicely adolescent, then,' I said.

'Oxymoron,' said Rohini.

'Clever-clogs,' I said. 'My sister's just like you.'

'As wise as she is beautiful? Heavily moustached?'

I laughed out loud. 'A know-all. And about as tactful.'

'Not fair. I've been tact itself, today.'

'Apart from telling Alice she's vain and spoilt and stupid.'

'Consider my restraint. I only remarked on it once,

and she's all of those things all the time. Plus I've been good all along about not mentioning the skull shrine, specially since it's probably the most interesting thing on the island, for me.'

I'd not mentioned the skulls, of course, so as not to frighten the ickles, but I'd made sure not even to think about them. 'Rohini, how long d'you think they've been there?'

'No idea, because one, I didn't see them and two, the crabs could strip a head down to bone in a day or two.'

'The crabs probably don't go up so far,' I said. But you could've gone up to look if you weren't so idle, I thought.

'I'll go, one of these days,' she said.

I avoided her eye: she knew what I'd been thinking.

'Never mind that,' she said. 'I've got a problem.'

'Umm?'

'The search for Rosie's man. It didn't yield a man, as you know.'

'But . . .'

'It did yield this.' She produced a small, damp paper bag and put it down between us. I opened it. Inside was a new packet of pills. In bubble-strips, none of them used. I didn't recognise the name so I read the information leaflet.

'For heart conditions,' I said. 'Not likely to belong to girls between eleven and eighteen.'

'Nor to anyone not called Dr William Montgomery.'

I turned the packet over. That was the name on the prescription label. And the date on the label was only a week old.

'So he must have been on the plane, you reckon? Doesn't mean he came off it. The pills could just have been blown by the gale.'

'They're very dry inside. More like they were carried in a pocket.'

'We don't know that. What's the problem, exactly?'

'Should we keep searching for him and the others there may be? Just the older girls?'

'Why just the older girls?'

'Imagine the squeaking if the ickles find rotting, putrefying bodies.'

It was shocking. She could have said it another way. She got on my nerves. Why doesn't she soften things? Her bluntness made me quarrelsome.

'Are you unpleasant on purpose?' I said.

'Oh, sometimes,' she said. 'Like everyone. But not just then. What annoyed you?'

'You needn't have said rotting, putrefying bodies. It sounded aggressive.'

'Wasn't meant to be.'

'Sounded it.'

'Are we going to bicker, or weave sunhats?' she said.

'Can't we bicker *and* weave sunhats?' I said.

We wove, for a bit.

'We could be bickering because I'm frightened,' she offered. 'I'm probably aggressive when I'm frightened.'

'*Probably*?' I said.

'Just a guess. Not much to go on. Haven't been frightened much.'

Her concession required a concession in return. 'I'm probably frightened too,' I offered back.

Pause. We wove some more.

'Now you ask me what I'm frightened of,' she said.

'Do I? I thought we were just doing a ritual making-up.'

She clicked her tongue impatiently. 'Social interactions baffle me. Mostly. Like conventions in history of art, which I learn without believing. The weasel in the foreground is telling us that Leonardo's mother-in-law has a cold, his central heating is on the blink, and he's appealing to the patronage of St Unlikely of Urbino.'

'What are you frightened of, Rohini?'

'Maybe the man is still alive. And well. And hiding.'

That chilled me. 'Why would he do that?'

'No idea. I don't like it when I have no idea.'

'Not a usual problem for you.'

'Is that a friendly tease, or a malicious dig?'

'Neither of the above. I'm appealing to the patronage of St Unlikely of Urbino. Listen, they'll rescue us soon, won't they? And then it won't matter about the man. We can just tell them about the pills. And come to think of it, with a heart condition, the crash is almost bound to have killed him. Realistically.'

'The rescue thing also frightens me. They should have come by now. Surely. With the electronic equipment they've got – they shouldn't just lose the plane to start with. And having lost us, they should quickly be able to find us. There are satellites all over the place up there. Surely?'

'For sure. But meanwhile, we're doing all we can.'

'Are we? A bigger fire? A fire in a different place?'

We both turned and looked up, in the direction of the crest of the island. We couldn't see it for the canopy of trees. 'It's a heck of a way up there,' I said. 'And people'd have to stay with it, otherwise it'd go out.'

'Maybe we should, though.'

'I'm worried about something else,' I said. 'The baby. It makes no sense that Debs does it all. It's really hard work.'

'Not to mention her lady-in-waiting duties.'

'Shouldn't we do something?'

'Exactly what? Alice has spoken. Alice never changes her mind. Alice hasn't got a mind to change, just a set of whims backed up by a Death Stare.'

'Death Stare?'

Rohini scowled at me fiercely. It was a crap imitation, but I knew what she meant. 'Just because she doesn't like something . . .' I protested.

'OK. You tell her. You're the one who doesn't like conflict.'

'No one likes conflict.'

'Alice does.'

From the Island

A week later . . .

CHAPTER EIGHT

Emma, 17, 5'10", blonde hair: During the rest-time, when the sun was hottest, Rohini and I sat near the baggage. We'd done it the second time because we'd done it the day before, then by the third time we did it because we'd always done it. Time closed behind us like a heavy curtain. The trees hung over us like an old-fashioned ballet set. And the sun beat down.

Most of the others were asleep, I assumed. A little way down the beach, towards the clearing, Fliss's grave was a mound of flowers. The ickles decorated the grave every day, the crabs looted it every night, and Rohini restored it very early every morning. Just beyond the grave, three ickles were doing Nadia's bug dance – *Another bug bites the sand, squish. Another bug bites the sand, squash.*

Nadia's good with the ickles. One morning, they got a craze for chanting the Queen song and stamping. Susan, who's blind as a bat without her contact lenses but tries to pretend she isn't, tripped and fell. They modulated the song to *Another one bites the dust – JUMP!* When they said jump, they landed on Susan, who by this time was crying (she cries a lot). Anneka was trying to stop them, but Nadia just started doing her bug dance beside them and the temptation to join her drew them, one by one. Since then it's become an ickles pastime.

We'd be left alone today, I guessed. For the previous few days, the ickles had taken to coming up to us one by one during rest-time. Sometimes for reassurance – the can't bird *is* just a bird, isn't it? Tamsin says there's ghosts, that's silly, isn't it? The grown-ups will come to get us, won't they? They haven't forgotten us, have they? – sometimes for mediation in their squabbles – she took it, no I didn't, yes you did, it was your fault, no it wasn't, yes it was – sometimes for minor first aid, which Rohini doled out from the medicine cache she kept in the jungle somewhere. And sometimes just to be with us because we were the nearest to adults they had.

Yesterday Tamsin'd stationed herself between us and the clearing, just out of earshot, and tackled any ickle heading in our direction. We didn't know what she said to them but they'd all turned back. We'd seen it, and we'd not discussed it much. I don't know Rohini's reason: mine was because I thought I knew the answer, that Tamsin was doing what Debs told her, stopping the ickles talking to us, because any power we got was less power for Alice. I really think they care about power, stupid as it seems. And that issue was a can I didn't want to open. Or think about, now.

'It's been a week,' I said.

'A week and a day,' said Rohini.

'Over a week since we crashed. A week since we

first sat here at this time making leaf-hats. We should have a leaf-hat mountain by now. We would have, if any of the ickles could hang on to one for more than five minutes. Or learn how to make them. Or if they were more durable. As it is —'

'As it is we shall soon have stripped the entire island of vegetation, like the giant panda eating itself into extinction.'

'Hyperbole.'

Our grumbling was disingenuous. I knew it as we did it. It was (certainly for me, probably for Rohini) a relief to have something to do which was evidently useful. Particularly since the sunblock had run out.

'It would've helped if they'd kept the least grip on the sunblock. And if Alice hadn't fraudulently converted both tubes I gave Debs for the baby,' said Rohini. She'd read my mind. I'd found her doing it more and more often. It was disconcerting. As if time was accelerating, as if we were already a long-married couple.

'At least Debs can keep the baby in the shade. Better than we can control the ickles.' I was being optimistic: I felt it was my role. An optimistic second-in-command, a lady-in-waiting. I was trained into that by my sister Christie. She's only a year older than me but because she was so brilliant she kept skipping grades, in America, and then again back in England, so she ended up going to Cambridge when she was sixteen. And since both of us went to boarding schools for some of our education we weren't together all that often. But when we were small she'd always been the one with the ideas and I'd been the one who helped carry them out – or, since she wasn't always that practical, actually carried them out. And picked up the pieces afterwards. She'd taken the dizzy/sensitive space – I was left sensible Emma. She was also mercurial, with moods of black despair sometimes. So I got into the role of utterer-of-bracing-good-hope. Rohini wasn't prone to moods as far as I could see, but she was much more shuttered than Christie, and by now I knew that I only saw as much of what she was feeling as she wanted me to see. Which wasn't usually much at all. Still, the optimistic role seemed to have stuck.

And that left Rohini playing the pessimist. 'Debs *could* keep the baby in the shade. But she doesn't always.'

'She does most of the time.'

'It doesn't look very well to me. It's thinner and its eyes are sunk into its head.'

'He's bound to be pining for his mother, and there's been a change in diet . . . We're all looking thinner. We've all got the runs.'

'Don't I know it. All over the island,' said Rohini. 'They could have used the latrines. But oh no, "*I can't use that smelly place, yuk it smells, there's lots of island, I'm not going where there's other people's poo, eeuch.*"' She was putting on an ickles voice, high-pitched, mindless, whiny, supplicating. '"*Alice doesn't use it, why should we? That's treating us like second-class citizens, that's volilating health and safety, I'll sue, I'll show you, see if I don't.*"' Now it was a Tamsin voice, brash, accusing. She went on in her own, 'Doesn't it make you want to . . .' She tailed off.

'It makes me want to fricassee Tamsin's mother,' I said.

'And Alice's Dads. And Susan's bloody horse.' She tore her current leaf-hat into viciously small pieces and scattered them over her lap. 'But that's just irritation, I suppose, because we're all cooped up together. All the same, if they're not going to use the latrines, I wish they'd stop banging on about the environment. They can't even pronounce it, most of them.'

'It wouldn't matter if they couldn't pronounce it if they at least protected it,' I said.

'A message from Miss Smug from the planet Sententious,' she said, with a smile to temper the sting.

'Fair enough,' I said. I wouldn't fall out with her, and she had a point. 'Don't worry about the baby being ill, that's all. We're none of us a hundred per cent.'

'You may be right.' She sounded unconvinced. 'I'm not an authority on babies. I don't like them.'

'I know. You told me.'

'Did I? When?'

'At Heathrow. At the press conference.'

Silence. I was thinking of that other world. Rohini began to laugh.

'What is it?' I said.

'The competition man, Ken Wright. With his exploitative scam. Lots of photogenic young girls, cheap. Now he's killed them all, as far as the world knows.'

I laughed too, to cover the chill underneath. 'Boy, is he on a downer for his publicity . . . Rohini, why did you enter the competition in the first place?'

'I didn't. My cousin Kavita did.'

I was taken aback. 'Do you mean you didn't write the essay thing? On women in Hinduism?' I was disappointed. I liked what she'd written. I'd actually thought hers was the only interesting one. The others were platitudes, really. Mine was, though mine was marginally better written than most.

'Oh, I *wrote* it,' she said.

'What d'you mean, then?'

'Did you really think the competition was what we wrote, or drew, or painted?'

'Yes,' I said, an inch away from being huffy. This detached leading-me-on, *I*-know-*you*-don't type thing was an affectation of hers. It would have annoyed me if I'd allowed it to, which I didn't. On the island, Rohini stood between me and . . .

I didn't want to consider the and.

'Are you going to explain?' I said.

'The competition was the *photographs*,' she said. 'Of course it was. What we *looked* like. Because everything depends on that. The TV ads, the newspaper stuff, the website coverage. With appropriate ethnic representation: two blacks, one brown, one Chinese. As many blondes as possible. One token redhead.'

I was very hurt. 'I liked Nadia's painting,' I said.

'So did I. They were lucky there. A good-looking redhead who'll probably be able to paint one day.'

I finished one leaf-hat, started another. I waited for her to say something about my essay. Which had been well written, I thought. It *had*.

After the silence had stretched far enough to make it evident that Rohini had little understanding of the obligations of friendship, I said, 'What'd you think of mine, then?'

Rohini looked at me sideways. She was laughing at me. 'Never ask a question if you're not confident of the answer,' she said. In her quotation voice.

'Don't quote at me,' I snapped.

'What did *you* think of it?' she said.

'I really meant it,' I said. 'When I wrote it. Then I felt embarrassed.'

'Why?'

'Mostly because my English teacher raved about it. Which is usually a contra-indication . . . Why d'you think Debs won't give salt to the baby?'

'She says it's bad for them,' said Rohini in a neutral voice.

If it'd been me, I'd've been annoyed. It stood to reason the baby needed salt, since all the rest of us used the salt-pots Rohini had set up. It was a really good idea, I thought. She'd read somewhere that losing salt was a problem when you sweated, and we weren't sure at all anyway about what we were eating, and we were sweating a lot. So she suggested collecting seawater and evaporating it. The goody-goods had found big stones with dips in them and they were now salt-pots. We took salt when we wanted and everybody did, even Debs. But she wouldn't give it to the baby.

More silence. 'If the competition was all about how you look, what about Debs, then?' I said. 'Why did they pick her? She's not exactly . . .'

'She won under a different heading. She's a woman of courage. Her mother's ill, Debs has to look after swarms of siblings. Remember, it was a separate section. You had to be nominated by someone else.'

'I never read the rules all through, only my bit.'

'It was different, anyway. And I expect they didn't get many nominations, and most of those would've been children with disabilities. Not that easy to move about. Or necessarily that tempting to take pictures of.'

'What about the aaah factor?'

'More commonly the yuk factor. They were probably grateful to find someone halfway normal-looking.'

I couldn't keep myself from saying what was on my mind, though I hadn't meant to. 'So you cheated, in the competition,' I said.

'No I didn't. I read the rules carefully. It said send a photograph. Not a photograph of yourself, just a photograph. So I did. I sent a photo of Kavita. Could've sent a photo of Nelson Mandela as far as the rules *said*. What they meant was quite another thing.'

'What happened when you had to go to London to make the telly ads?'

'They saw I wasn't the same person, of course. Unless I'd lost height and gained weight and rearranged my face. But I pointed out their own phraseology, and they cut their losses. You may have noticed I wasn't used in any of the ads.'

'I just thought I'd missed the ones with you in . . . All the same, I don't understand why you actually came on the trip. It doesn't seem your sort of thing.'

'Research,' she said.

'What sort of research?'

'I'm doing it as a project.'

'For A Level? Surely you've finished your exams?'

'For my university course. I thought I could use it somewhere. Primary research.'

'So you'll be studying travel and tourism, then?'

'Archaeology and anthropology.'

'And the competition winners are your subjects.'

'And you're annoyed with me. Why?'

'I don't think we count as anthropology anyway. We're not primitive,' I said, too annoyed with her to discuss it. Hurt because she hadn't said anything complimentary about my essay, which was the least she could do. Put down by being lumped with the others as a subject for superior Rohini's study. Then, even through my annoyance, I caught her eye. 'What're you giggling at?'

'D'you reckon the Britneys are highly evolved?'

'They're children,' I said. 'That age. They're always like that in a gang. They're almost normal human beings, one to one. They just need handling.'

'The prefect speaks . . . Did you go to boarding school?'

'Some of the time.'

'And were you a prefect?'

'Yes.'

'So tell me what's wrong with the kids.'

'What d'you mean?'

'They don't *do* anything.'

'They do things for Alice,' I said. 'They built her a shelter.'

'The goody-goods built her a shelter. The ickles pretended to help. And otherwise they sit around with what's left of the magazines, doing the quizzes over and over again — such stupid quizzes. "What's your snoggability rating?" They groom each other endlessly, like monkeys. Pass around the mirror and squeal at their spots. Wash their hair. Tell each other the same lies about GUYS. Slurp over the pull-out posters of the guys in BOY BANDS, who all look like girls to me.'

'That's because you're an OLDER WOMAN.'

'They've got the whole island to explore and they sit in heaps in the same places.'

'That's what they'd have done at home. It's partly physical. Adolescent lethargy.'

'And they play seriously unpleasant tricks on Susan.'

'They don't mean them nastily,' I said, disingenuously, because I was afraid they did.

'It's the lack of intention that worries me. Not nasty intention, but any intention. Or any sense of responsibility, or consequences, or — or *sense*. They jump out at Susan and say *Whoooo, I'm a skull*, and she can't see them and thinks they are, each time, and she screams and whinnies, and then Anneka tells her it's only one of the ickles, and she feels better, and is freshly surprised the next time she hears *Whoooo, I'm a skull*. Repeat da capo. And they don't read books. We've plenty of books. They don't want them.'

'Because you can't read books in groups.'

'But why do they *want* to be in groups?'

'Because they're that age. Didn't you?

'Absolutely not.'

'You must have had friends.'

'Of course. One at a time, or two at the most. We

never groomed. And we were past playing games.'

We sat without talking, watching the robber cycle the birds went through. A middle-sized bird hovered, then dived and emerged with a living fish flapping in its beak. Then the bird made for shore, presumably to its nest, maybe to feed its young. Meanwhile a bigger bird with an impressive wing span would be circling above, biding its time to swoop down and steal the fish. And then, sometimes, when the larger bird was devouring its spoil, the crabs would try to steal it, and sometimes they succeeded. And then, sometimes, a huge grey-white eel would slither out of the sea and devour the crabs.

'Are we still missing things from the baggage?' I said.

'Yes. A little more each day.'

'They're bound to take the clothes, really. And it's partly a game for them, to see if they can do it without being spotted.'

'I don't think it's just the ickles.'

'Who then? Alice and Debs?' I couldn't see the rest of us doing it. The goody-goods wouldn't dream of it. Nadia spent every private moment drawing, on any scraps of paper she could find, and sometimes on the sand when she needed space. Rouchelle and Tawheeda kept themselves to themselves most of the time, and Tawheeda hardly ever spoke, but they were easy to get along with. Plus they worked hard. They'd taken over the food side, collecting and cooking. I'd seen no sign of them dressing up.

'Not Alice and Debs,' said Rohini.

'The crabs?' We'd all got used to the crabs swarming,

particularly at night, tearing things apart, scutting away to their hidden places, mostly under rocks. 'The birds?'

'Couldn't possibly be,' she said flatly.

'What aren't you telling me?' I said. There'd been something in her voice.

'It's the things that're missing,' she said.

'Like what?'

'Like a CD player. Headphones. CDs. Books.'

'What's the point of a CD player? We've got no batteries.'

'Yes we have. I took them out and stockpiled them. Just in case.'

And she hadn't told me. Thanks a lot for your confidence, Rohini. 'Just in case of what?' I snapped.

'I don't know. I don't know,' she said. 'Anyway, some of them have gone too. The ones that fit the player. The missing CDs are classical, as well. And the books are non-fiction. A travel guide to the South Pacific, and some heavyweight novels.'

'I never saw those,' I said. Our library was stocked with beach fiction, as far as I'd seen, and largely untouched by the ickles, though they had kept passign round the one with the really explicit sex scene on pages 108–9 until those pages fell out. Then they just read the pages till they disintegrated.

'I only saw them the first time I sorted through. I was looking forward to the travel guide. We're in the South Pacific, for sure, and it might've been useful. Then when I went back, it'd gone. Plus the serious novels.'

Suddenly, I ached for a proper book. 'What novels?'

'Some Proust. Dostoevsky. Flaubert. The kind of

books people keep promising themselves they'll read, and take on holiday, and bring back unopened. I'd've opened them, though.'

'So would I,' I said. Books. Real books . . . 'Was the Proust in translation?'

'Yes. *Swann's Way*. Not the first one.'

'Better than nothing, though.'

The books, for a moment, were all I wanted. They'd materialised in my mind and then been snatched away. It was like thinking, all right I'll go to see a certain film, nothing much better to do, and then when you can't get in, it becomes the thing you most wanted to see, ever.

'So?' said Rohini. 'Who d'you reckon could have taken them?'

I had no idea. 'And you think they were taken the first night?'

'The travel guide, certainly. Some of the books.'

'Must have been the ickles,' I said, though I didn't believe it. 'They're like jackdaws. They'd take things, doesn't matter what, just to put one over on us.'

'Such glittery-glittery things for them to take,' said Rohini.

She was right, of course. They'd never choose those . . . 'If they took them at night, maybe they couldn't see what they were getting.'

Rohini clicked her tongue against her teeth in dismissal. That mannerism of hers irritated me even more than her quotation voice. Then I took a grip on myself and remembered how irritating I could be, Pollyanna-ing all over the shop. Other people were bound to be irritating, cooped up with them like this.

And Rohini had one great characteristic that made up for everything in this situation. She never whined.

'Who do you think it is, then?' I asked.

'You don't want to talk about it, do you?' she said.

'Not unless we can do something about it,' I admitted. 'What can we do about it?'

'We won't know what to do about it until we work out who it is.'

This wrangle could go on for ever. I didn't want to think about it, and I'd just spoiled another leaf-hat. I wanted to go to sleep and I didn't want to keep talking about this. I looked around for any distraction, and found an excellent one. 'What are they doing out there?' I pointed at an astonishing sight – Alice and Debs standing in the lagoon. They were talking to each other. The baby was on Debs's back as usual, in a sling, in the full sun. They were just talking. Alice never even stood up unless to show off, or do the exercises she'd set herself from a fitness maintenance programme in one of the magazines. She never stood in the sun: no dark glasses, she'd get squint-wrinkles.

'Rohini – what do you think they're doing?'

'No idea.'

'Has anything happened?'

'Not that I know of.'

She wasn't playing my game: I hadn't played hers.

Anneka, 11, 5'1", mousy hair: After rest-time Susan and I went exploring, up towards the volcano. I wanted to, she didn't so much, because not being able to see it's quite hard for her to move about, but she doesn't like sitting still any more than I do. And I tell her about what I see, so tho it's not as good as if she could see it herself it's better than staying on the beach all the time where the other kids tease us. Actually they mostly tease *her* now, because she's such an easy target.

We'd just found some caves which looked promising when we heard Rohini's alarm thing. I thought, rescue. They've come. Weird, I was almost disappointed. I wanted them to come but not yet. In a way, I like the island. It's a new place to be, a new start, and I get on all right here. I don't whinge and I don't complain and Tawheeda says I'm the best tree-climber and I do things, I haven't just fallen apart like some of them. When Tamsin isn't there I get on all right with most of the ickles, and all the older ones cept Alice and Debs. Best of all, Susan's the first actual friend I've ever had. I like being with Susan.

She thought it was rescue too, and she started waving her arms in the air and jumping up and down, and crying, but it was with happiness. She didn't think of me. So I didn't say my feelings – better not. I climbed on a rock where I could see down to the beach outside the clearing, and there weren't any rescuers, just the kids going into the clearing, so it wasn't rescue after all. And now I felt awful about that, because I'd been so sure we were leaving, and now I was frightened we'd never leave.

I told Susan. She cried some more. I held her hand until she stopped. Then we went down the hill as quickly as we could.

The meeting'd started. And Alice was taking it. That was even weirder than me not wanting to go home yet. She always wants to be in charge of meetings but she can never think of anything to say so she lets Rohini get on with it and then grumbles at what she says. But this time she was standing right in the middle and spouting all sorts of stuff about how great the island was and how lucky we were to be on it and how she really liked looking at the sunrise and the sunset and the plants and the butterflies. And how we'd got to care for the environment.

Then she went on to how we must do things and occupy ourselves and make the most of the time, all the stuff that Rohini and Emma have being saying from the start, and that she hasn't been listening to. And not letting anyone else listen to either. Unless it was something she wanted, like the shelter that Vanessa and Charlotte and Mei Lin built for her, and then rebuilt twice because it wasn't right the first two times.

Susan and me went into the clearing – all the others were there – and apologised for being late and sat down at the end of a log with the other kids, and Alice gave us her smile, which I actually think is more scary than her Death Stare because she *so* doesn't mean it but you don't know what she does mean.

Hi, Anneka, hi, Susan, glad you can be with us, she said. (What? She's using the grown-ups' I'm-good-with-kids voice. Who's she trying to impress?)

Hi, we both said.

So what I was saying was, we will be rescued but we don't know when, and until then, we must make the most of it, mustn't we?

Yes, Alice, yes, Alice, everyone said. I don't know why the kids like her, but they do. They're afraid of her as well, but they like her to like them.

So I want to hear some ideas, for us to make the most of it, she said. Any ideas?

There was one of those silences.

It was good when we dressed up and danced, said Tamsin. We could dress up again. And practise our dances. And paint our faces.

I liked the memorial service, said Vanessa.

Me too, me too, people said, and not just Charlotte and Mei Lin.

We need help with the food, Rouchelle said.

And with collecting wood for the fire . . . we use so much wood . . . it really needs to dry, we have to go higher up for it now and it's really soaked under the leaves . . . said the three friends.

No me-toos for either of those, no surprises. Susan and me always help.

Alice was going to say something but we never found out what it was because of the noise. Suddenly, really loud music was playing, orchestra music. I'd heard it before, but never on the island, of course. Parrots started flying and squawking and some of the kids screamed.

What is it? What is it? said Alice.

Beethoven's Fifth, said Rohini and Emma together, as if they'd practised.

Alice gave them a Death Stare. You know I don't mean that, she said. Where's it coming from, what's MAKING THAT NOISE?

It was coming from the jungle, further down towards the baggage, but not that far away.

The kids started squealing and crying. Alice stood there with her jaw dropped open. Rohini shouted,

QUIET, SHUT UP! EVERYBODY COME WITH ME!

Rohini, 17, 5'2", black hair: The missing CD player. We have to find the source of the sound. I hate running, I'm very slow, and most of them overtake me on the sand and plunge into the jungle. By the time I get there they're standing around watching the machine, still blasting out music.

Emma presses stop. Parrots squawk. I look about. No sign of anyone, but then there wouldn't be: there'd been no sign of anyone for over a week, but he'd been there. Somewhere.

From the Island

They'll never find me. They'll never look up.

I survived the crash, I escaped the plane, I survived the swim across the lagoon in the storm and the scramble across the beach. All for nothing: I'll be dead, rescued or not, in under a week.

At least now they know I'm here I can stop pretending to be the island. I'd run out of material. You'd think, after six years of post-graduate education, I'd know *something* about the South Pacific, but no, I was entirely dependent on the travel book. It was dull. My imagination was dry.

The first day, I didn't wake till late afternoon. I felt deathly ill. I managed to get water and food. I'd lost my pills. I heard the light chatter and wails of the girls, climbed a tree, concealed myself. I was so bruised that nowhere would have been comfortable, and I felt safe in the tree.

By the evening I felt a little better, and explored, only to realise who I was marooned with. I simply could not bear the prospect of joining them. Twenty or so adolescent girls, all wanting to talk about themselves. It wouldn't matter that I'm old. I possess two ears, and I'm breathing, and I will remind them of their grandfathers or grandfathers they have seen on television or just the grandfathers they feel they deserve. Lo, a disaster occurs to little Jane; lo, she must talk about it. Again. And again. And again.

I've earned the right to disengagement. I began my career as a priest, lost my faith (and my patience), tided myself over financially as a poet (not a good one, but popular, especially with women, and an efficient self-publicist), and then took up psychology. I've been married twice. I've had several lovers. I've been listening to women all my life. Enough, already.

Dropping the CD player was an accident. I was comfortably installed up my tree, listening to a (mediocre) version of the Beethoven through a (mediocre) set of headphones, when a parrot flew past and startled me. I jumped, dislodged the player, and it fell to the ground, detaching itself from the headphones. Which made the music audible, especially since hitting the ground didn't silence it as you'd expect, but affected the volume control. It was stunningly loud.

I moved away immediately and reinstalled myself in another tree, well hidden by foliage. I don't move quickly (I'm seventy, with a heart condition) but I had plenty of time.

When they came, they argued. It was getting dark, and eventually most of them went back to the fire, though the Indian persisted in trying to organise a search. She was left only with the tall good-looking blonde one: not enough. They looked, but neither looked up. Then they went away, leaving me in peace, to reflect on my final enterprise.

My final enterprise is suicide. My heart is now so inefficient that my consultant recommends a by-pass. I don't want an operation. I don't want to creep around, pills clanking inside me. The youngest of my children is now twenty-seven, and though she still isn't in any sense mature, neither is my eldest (forty-two); nor, for that matter, am I.

My suicide plan was simple. I've always wanted to see Ayers Rock, or so my family believe. Possibly once I said I did. If so, I've forgotten why, but the idea was firmly established in their minds, so when I said I was going to climb Ayers Rock, they clucked about taking it slowly in my state of health. But it was a familiar concept to them; they didn't object. The strongest objection came from my youngest, who said if I was going to climb it I must show respect by calling it by its Aborigine name.

I bought the first available ticket to Australia. First class. If I'd been in my seat for the crash I'd have been killed with the rest of the first-class passengers, and perhaps that would have been easiest. In fact I was (inconsistently) trying to avoid deep-vein thrombosis by walking up and down the plane, and when the turbulence started I strapped myself in right at the back, among the girls.

I'd thought we'd be rescued immediately. By the next morning it was too late, I thought, to join them. I had books, some music. I had my death to look forward to. Death soon palled as a focus for meditation, I must in fairness say. I began to be interested, almost against my will, in the girls. Not as individuals, at first, but in the group dynamics. I pretended to myself there was a story. I'd thought I wanted to be alone, but I didn't. I wanted to take part.

On the other hand, I didn't want to be known. So I became the Island, sentient but inanimate, detached, there but not there. (A description of me frequently screamed by my second wife.) I watched them from a distance, and mined the travel guide for local colour. I even started observing the actual island's flora and fauna. The last time I took up natural history was after I was given a toy microscope for my eighth birthday. That interest wanted after a day: as did this. I only managed to spot two varieties of spider, both unappealing. See one parrot, as far as I'm concerned, and you've seen them all.

Which brings us up to date. My current position is much more blameworthy. They know someone is here. They may well be frightened. I should make myself known to them, allay their fears, make up an explanation for not coming forward before.

I could join them, then deliberately alienate them, of course. But in my present weakened condition, and after forty years of nodding and affirming for a living, I doubt if I could keep it up. I'd lose concentration and relapse into the formula of repeating their own words, which they almost invariably mistake for sympathetic understanding.

At least I'm too old for them to dress up for me, surely.

Guilt is unnecessary. What can happen to them? There are no boys to fight over. I insist on having privacy before I die, which I certainly will, soon, without my pills. Particularly since now they know someone's here, they'll be watching out. The strain of avoiding them, alone, will probably kill me.

CHAPTER NINE

Rohini, 17, 5'2", black hair: Emma and I search. We find nothing. On the way back to the fire and the others, she says, 'Sorry. You were right about the man. I should've listened to you.'

I'm pleased, not so much by her acknowledging an obvious truth as by the warmth of her tone. 'Forget it,' I say. 'Now *I'll* tell *you* how to look on the bright side. If we have to have a Significant Other lurking about, at least he's got a heart condition. If he threatens us, we'll just send in Alice the Warrior Queen. One look at the bod and he'll be so excited he'll pop off.'

'Or we can send in Tamsin to demand her inviolable right to bore him to death about her mother.'

We're still inventing silly scenarios and laughing about them when Rouchelle comes up the beach to meet us. When she's a few yards away she stands square on, barring our way. She doesn't smile. We stop.

'Hi?' says Emma.

'Hi,' says Rouchelle, flatly, warningly. 'If you're coming to join us, you better apologise, Rohini. Apologise to us. Alice's seriously angry, and we all are.'

'What on earth about? What is this?' says Emma.

'It was scary. The ickles were scared. That's not fair,' says Rouchelle. There's fear in her own voice still.

'I'm sorry,' I say, not knowing why it's my fault, not wanting to make a bad situation worse. 'I –'

Rouchelle goes on as if I haven't spoken. 'You gotta apologise, major league.'

'I just did,' I say, baffled.

'Not like that. To all of us. Alice says maybe even write it down and read it out, and then we can put the apology up on a tree so everyone can read it whenever they want. Or maybe read it out at the memorial service.'

'What memorial service?' says Emma. 'And what exactly is Rohini apologising for?'

'It was Debs worked it out. You kept back things from the baggage, yeah? Then you played a joke on us. A crap joke. It was you. There's no one else. It was you with the CD player, that you kept for yourself.'

'That's not true,' I say.

'Debs said you'd say that. Look, joke's over, OK? Just fit in, OK? Just do what the rest of us want, for once, OK, instead of ordering us about? I think the joke stinks but I'm doing you a favour, warning you that we've all sussed it. I thought you needed warning, OK? Just be told. Things could get ugly back there.' She jerks her head towards the fire.

I open my mouth to say something, but Emma waves me silent. 'Thanks, Rouchelle,' she says. 'Thanks very much.'

'No big deal,' says Rouchelle, and walks away from us, back to the others.

Emma and I look at each other. 'No way,' I say. 'Confirm their delusions? No way.'

'They've made it up because they're scared.'

'I know that.'

'It's safer for them to deny that there's anyone else here.'

'Short-term, maybe. But there *is* someone else, and I'm not going to lie.'

So we join the others and I don't lie and there's a profoundly stupid row, during which I try to explain and they try not to listen They achieve their objective, I don't.

The upshot is that they forbid me to sleep near the fire. I'm quite prepared to settle down near the fire anyway and let them move me by force – by now I'm angry too – but Emma the Conciliator comes with me a little way off, talking to me soothingly as if I'm an animal or a baby, there there, take it easy, it'll look different tomorrow.

The facts won't be different tomorrow, I say, but I let myself be persuaded because under my anger I think it really would be better sorted out in the morning, in the light of day, when everyone's calmed down.

Emma and I talk a while before we settle, at first about other things, mostly about the stars. I'm still a little angry but she's deeply upset, and it ends up with *me* trying to reassure *her*. All the talking round the fire's stopped by the time I go to sleep.

I wake in the early hours from a deep, deep sleep. At first I think I'm dreaming, then I think I've been woken by the crabs and try to see them. No crabs.

The noise is Debs and Emma, talking. Then Debs goes away. I'm still half asleep. 'What is it?' I say.

'Nothing. Debs wants me to have the baby for the rest of the night. About time someone else took a turn.'

I don't even really process the information. I'm just grateful to be able to sink away again into a dark mindless place with no stupid girls in it.

Emma, 17, 5'10", blonde: It was the worst thing that'd ever happened to me. When I look back now my life is split into two parts: before that waking-up, and after it.

I realised very quickly, unusually for me. I'm a slow comer-to-consciousness. My family tease me for it. But I knew somehow, even asleep, that I was in charge of the baby, so my first thought was, why isn't he crying? He usually started to grizzle at dawn, and this was later than dawn.

Then I looked at him and knew. He wasn't grizzling because he was dead. Not breathing. Almost stiff. Dead.

I kept still and thought. Had I suffocated him? I didn't think I'd rolled over. I was still in the same position, more or less, and he was wrapped in a pashmina lying beside my face. I hadn't done anything, that was what I'd done. I'd not saved his life. I'd not known he was slipping away because I'd been asleep. He'd died alone . . . I'd have to tell everyone. I'd have to tell Debs. She'd looked after him for over a week and he was fine. Then I'd looked after him just for a few hours, and he'd died.

No one else seemed to be awake yet. I woke up Rohini and told her.

'Oh, shit,' she said.

'The poor baby,' I said. I couldn't bear to look at him.

'Debs's dumped you in it,' said Rohini. 'She gave you a dead baby.'

'She *wouldn't* have done.'

'She has. Did you check he was alive when you got him?'

'Of *course* not . . . She said he was asleep, not to disturb him.'

'So you don't know for sure he was breathing?'

'No,' I said. Not relieved, because I don't think anything could relieve me of that guilt. More thinking about Rohini's suggestion. No, I didn't know for sure when the baby had died. I knew for sure I was going to get the blame for it, and that I felt the responsibility.

Debs, 16, 5'5", dyed blonde: Some of the cameras've gotta be in the trees by the pool, stands to reason. There'll be plenty everywhere else, but there's gotta be some there. So I make sure posh-bitch Emma came to me there about the poor little sod, didn't I, and I got my faces ready, and my words. Surprised, upset, sweet as pie, poor you, not your fault, poor you. The others think I'm great, I can see, and they fuss round me, poor you, poor you. And round the baby, tho they don't like dead things.

Alice's ready, too. She's had all night to get her act together and to get the funeral sorted. Took a while to get it in her head that the diamante gear isn't on.

She isn't the brightest bean in the can but she's Miss In, and I'm with her. She gets it fast enough sometimes, like about the cameras, when I tell her, this has got to be the competition, right here, they crash us on an island with cameras all over and microphones and then they watch us 24/7. There can't be cameras and microphones in the lagoon so I take her out there to tell her, explain it, so when we get back to where they see and hear us they won't know we got it, they'll think we're being ordinary.

Alice catches on to that quick enough. She does acting classes, knows all about acting and the media, full of ideas. We've gorra play up to it, play nice, do things for the kids, make like we're enjoying ourselves and everything's great and the island's great and we love everyone, and laugh a lot, and keep our faces right, 24/7. Don't look bad when we wash, look good like model pictures, flash the merchandise. We're famous, I'll be rich. I'll get my breasts fixed first, or maybe my chin, and a proper dye job. Get a villa in Marbella, or maybe Torremolinos. Take the family. Get Mum some sun, maybe, she likes the sun. Get Haydon out of that lot he runs with. All of us together, double spreads in *Hello!*

I got this lot well sussed now. Bossy Paki – way out in the cold for the crap joke. Posh Bitch – baby-killer. Poor little sod dead, I wouldn't've wished it on him but kids are such a drag, don't I know, woman of courage, me.

Anneka, 11, 5'2", mousy hair: It was completely, totally, awfully awful about the baby. Poor him, poor

poor him, and POOR EMMA. He'd been looking sick, really really sick, before, and it wasn't Emma's fault, because she's absolutely brilliant in every way and she'd NEVER have done ANYTHING, NEVER . . . It was probly no salt for all this time, Emma said salt, and Debs wouldn't . . .

We buried the baby beside Fliss. Vanessa dug the grave and Alice put him in the ground, wrapped in the best pashmina, which she'd been using before. I tried not to but I did wonder if crabs eat pashmina.

Nearly all of us said or did something at the funeral. Alice ran it. She said she was taking the funeral of the Princess Diana of Wales as her theme. Susan couldn't say anything, she was crying too hard. Alice sang the Elton John song 'Daniel', she *said* cos the baby might have been called Daniel, but then I heard her tell Rouchelle that she'd learnt it as her talent for a beauty competition. She sang it OK. It was sad, actually. The kids sang 'Candle in the Wind'. I didn't, I didn't know it well enough, and it was a bit embarrassing cos neither did they. Rohini and Emma sang a song they said was Latin, cos they'd learnt it in their choirs at school. Sepratly, different schools. I could be in a choir when I get back, if I can find one. I don't think there's one at my school. They sang really well so I reckon if I'm in a choir I will too. I hope it isn't always in Latin cos I don't know any.

Tamsin's speech was quite long and I didn't get most of it. It was about us being Daniel's blood family (which we weren't) and about Daniel being the people's baby (Yeah, yeah, Debs said, the people's baby, then Alice joined in). Then Tamsin went on about what her mother says, that the best thing for a dead person is justice, and we'd all see that the dead baby got his rights. Compasation. Take it all the way to the High Court. She said it like question and answer, we'll see you get your rights, Daniel, and then we all had to say yes. You can get really tired of someone's mother if they come up all the time.

Tawheeda said the baby would be with his mother in heaven, and they would be laughing together now, safe in the arms of Jesus. I think she must be Christian. She finished with a prayer some of them knew that begins Our Father. I'd like to learn it. It would be even better if it was Our Grandfather but I spect I could change just that bit, it wouldn't matter.

When it came to me I just said, Goodbye, Baby, I'm sorry we didn't really know you because you were too young, and I'm sorry you've missed so much of your life, but that also means you'll miss the bad bits.

Nadia, 14, 5'6", redhead: After the funeral I was very tired, I don't know why, so I went to sleep during rest-time. I usually draw then because I can get a bit of peace. I woke up looking forward to getting back to the caves – I'm working on the bats now, there are hundreds and hundreds of them on the roofs of the caves like growths or ticks or clumps of leather, weird, interesting – but Alice called another meeting.

I don't know what's got into her since last night. Meetings, meetings, meetings up the bum. This one was to work out ways of having fun, she said. (I'm already having fun, or would be if I didn't have to go to meetings.) She said we'd meet every evening and talk about things, and she asked for suggestions for competitions and entertainment.

Emma said, how about a race to the ridge at the top of the island, with the younger ones starting first? She was getting at Alice cos Alice *so* wouldn't win it. I thought it was a waste of time, but Emma's OK and in deep doo-doo with the others now, so I said I was for it, and I teased the ickles into saying they were for it too. Alice said great, she'd be the judge. Rohini said, did we need a judge? If not, Alice could take part and not miss anything. Alice just looked past her, as if she wasn't there. She's been doing that ever since Rohini played the trick last night, and the younger ones are beginning to copy her.

Then Alice said, maybe not a race, maybe a competition everyone could win. Rohini said that wasn't a competition, it was a wank. Alice went red and said, Language! and one of the ickles said, What's a wank? and Rohini said, In Alice's case, everything she does and everything she says, and Tamsin said, You frightened us, you made us think you were a pedo, and the ickles all screamed, Pedo, pedo, and I don't think we'll be having a race to the ridge on top of the island.

After that I thought we'd be left alone, but Alice decided we'd have a competition with prizes for everyone. (Prize = banana.) The competition was for describing 'My most embarrassing moment'. That took a while and got repetitive towards the end cos everyone was cribbing their embarrassing moments from the same magazine. (I think Alice was going to crib as well: she looked annoyed when Rouchelle told hers and then said she wasn't taking part, she was judging.)

I don't know what happened after that. I'd stayed long enough. I made like I'd got the runs, and ran back to my bats.

Rohini, 17, 5'2", black hair: Now I'm being sent to Coventry by most of them. Surprising how irritating that can be, even when you don't want to talk to them in the first place. Perhaps not surprising. There's a big difference between 'I don't like you' and 'You don't like me'. Emma's very worried by my isolation, spending some of her time with me, some with them. Looking to build bridges, I suppose.

The embarrassing 'embarrassing moment' seems to last years. When it finally fizzles out I go alone back down to the baggage, sit where Emma and I always sit, and think. Two topics: 1) the man, 2) sudden change in Alice and Debs.

After some reflection, I settle the man question for the moment. He's been keeping out of our way this long, he probably doesn't mean us any harm, he'll keep. But he could do with his pills. I unearth them from my medicine stash (still undiscovered, apparently, as nothing's missing) and take them along to the place where we'd found the CD player. I balance them in a fork of a big tree, make them as obvious as possible, and whistle a few bars of Beethoven's Fifth to give him a clue.

No immediate response, but I didn't expect any. I go back to Emma's and my place, thinking she might have come to join me, but she hasn't. I can't see her on the beach, either. She must still be in the clearing with Alice and co.

I sit down again, hugging my knees. I'm not going to cry, but I could. Being upset doesn't help the thought processes, and though I wrestle with it, I can't make any sense of Alice and Debs's uncharacteristic burst of activity. It couldn't be connected with the death of the baby, because Alice had called her first meeting last night, and the baby was still alive then. Definitely. It was crying. Weakly. Poor little thing. Maybe I should have insisted on the salt. Or maybe salt *is* bad for babies, as Debs said.

It couldn't have been connected with the music incident, either, for the same reason: meeting before incident. Which leads me to the question of why everyone's decided, immediately, against my denial and against common sense, to believe that the music had been my joke. After Rouchelle's warning, when I'd gone in to explain and ended up the villain of a hysterical row, Alice had been the strongest proponent of the practical-joke case. But she's so thick she's never had an idea in her life. Debs thinks, Alice fronts it. Rouchelle had said something like that, anyway. Why would Debs blame me? 1) she really thought I'd done it, 2) she wanted to discredit me.

Paranoia. I'm not getting anywhere. My brain's woolly. Soon it'll be supper time and I'll have to face them out-facing me. It's so unjust. It isn't fair. I feel like an ickle. I want to whine and wail. I want to go home. For the first time since the crash, I almost sympathise with the ickles. I'd thought I was brave and they were cowardly, but me being brave had been easy. Maybe they feel all the time as I feel now, in which case they haven't been doing a bad job of getting on with it. Not a bad job at all. Whereas I've just coasted along, know-it-all Rohini, not organising the search that might have saved Fliss, not pushing the issue about the baby.

And now I'm splashing about in a swamp of self-pity, which never helps anyone.

The cure for which is not to waste time on what can't be changed, but to change the things that can. As my dadda would say. As I wish Dadda was here to say, then give me a hug. And Mamma, to joke with me. And Gran. Even Mohandas. I'd thought (never said to them, of course) that family took second place to friends, because I chose my friends. But right now what I want is family and hugs, not the cold faces of strangers blaming me because they're afraid.

Emma, 17, 5'10", blonde hair: I kept hoping the day would end, but time was going slower and slower. The memory of the dead baby was like a cold lump in my chest. Sometimes I could hardly breathe past it. Nothing as serious as this had ever happened to me before. Something you couldn't change, apologise for, put right. Non-negotiable. Even if Rohini was right and Debs had handed it over dead, somehow I was responsible. I was. Maybe because all the others thought so, and when all the others think something it takes shape and sits there, as real as truth.

Not all the others thought so, I kept saying to myself. Rohini didn't. But all the others thought Rohini had played the trick, and there wasn't a man at all, and that belief was so real also that it blurred Rohini's truth. Plus I didn't want to think about Rohini, because that was another lump-in-the-chest thing. She was being frozen out, so I couldn't go and sit with her and just be friends and talk about nothing, which was what I longed to do. I had to stay here in the clearing with Alice and Debs and some of the others and discuss what Alice called the Rohini Problem.

We'd been theoretically discussing it ever since the meeting, about half an hour now, but it hadn't been discussion, it had been Alice, emphatically rambling. About betrayal and what we all felt and I must feel it too, the joke had been too much, it wasn't even a joke, it was an evil trick and Rohini must make an apology, a *written* apology, and even then . . . But if the apology was written Rohini could read it out at the meeting, and then we could put it on a tree so everyone could read it, and it would be there so everyone could feel better, and . . . I must see, she (Alice) had the ickles to think of, and they mustn't be frightened by . . . The ickles were what mattered, I must *see* . . .

I only *saw* Alice, one side of me, all her stupid energy and her scowling will, pressing, pressing to get what she wanted, and Debs the other side, all spite and calculation, and the goody-goods nodding, yes, the ickles must be protected, yes, they mustn't be upset. And inside me the prospect of another meeting run by Alice congealed into yet a third lump of fear. If the lumps were on the outside I'd begin to look like that goddess, all tits.

The fear was worse because I was bewildered. Alice had never before shown the least interest in anything except herself. Her previous position on the ickles was that they must do what they like because, hey, we're all equal. Now suddenly she'd turned into Den Mother.

We'd made a sort of equilibrium, Rohini and me, on the island. It was ticking over. (Apart from the baby, oh lord, apart from the baby.) Now there was a man somewhere out there, Alice and Debs had metamorphosed, and Rohini was a spit away from being the victim of a pack.

Alice'd stopped talking. Just that was a pleasure, until I realised I'd been asked something I hadn't heard. 'Sorry?' I said.

'Tell her,' Alice said. 'Tell her what she's got to do. Tell her we're gonna have a meeting after supper, and she's gotta bring a written apology. And tell her to bring the rape-alarm thing, so I can call the meeting.'

'You won't need the rape alarm,' I said. 'We'll all be here having supper.'

'Whose side you on?' said Debs. 'You wanna take her side against the kids? The poor scared kids?'

'We've got to look after the ickles,' said Vanessa. 'We must look after the ickles.'

Christie has a saying: the less the sense, the more the conviction. I don't know if it's a quotation, but it's always annoyed me. Patronising, condescending, I'm brighter than you so I know better. Now I knew what she meant, and I wanted to say it, but there was no one to hear it and understand. Except Rohini. Who I had to get back to before I started to cry.

'I'll tell her,' I said.

Rohini, 17, 5'2", black hair: I knew something was very wrong with Emma by the way she walked. Usually, she has a spring in her walk, even on sand. She's tall and strong and proud of it, and every day she'd swum up and down the lagoon for over an hour to keep fit, and she'd told me that was nothing compared to her usual training which included weights and sprinting and at least two hours in the pool. Emma was the body beautiful, all the blessings of nature combined with self-discipline. Health and beauty. I'd teased her about it. Maybe I was just a bit jealous. No, amend that, certainly I was a lot jealous. But now watching her wallowing along like Vanessa, as if her leg muscles had turned to ribbon, I want to put the swagger back.

I'm not a demonstrative person outside the family, largely because I'm not sure how welcome the physical affection of a short, squat, moustached person might be. But I hug her anyway. She needs hugging. She clings on to me. I cling back. Not being familiar with the process, I take my lead from her. Eventually she lets me go, but it's a long time.

Then we sit down, she brushes away tears, and tells me what they'd said.

Blind rage, a gratifying emotion when justified, rushes through me. 'That's crap,' I say.

She snaps back. 'Of course it is. Why won't you bloody listen?'

'I *am* listening, and I say it's crap.'

'That's really, really helpful.'

'What do you want me to say?'

She waves a hand, pointlessly.

I have to make her see. 'A detailed apology for something I haven't done. A lie. It's – it's Galileo. Salem. Stalinist show-trials. McCarthy . . .'

'Trust you, trust *you* . . . bloody big issues . . . we're just girls, on an island, doing the best we can –'

'You are. I am. What Alice and Debs are up to, who the hell knows –'

'They say it's for the ickles –'

'It's really going to help the ickles, telling them lies –'

'But if it wasn't you, then there's a man –'

'So there's a man –'

'They won't *listen!*'

'Well I *won't lie!*'

We glare at each other.

'It's not for the ickles, anyway. It's a form of trans-ferred selfishness Alice and Debs are using. It's for the kids, it's for the kids. People do it all the time. It's just an excuse to get what they want, but if you use kids as a sacred weapon it silences the argument. The kids. Aaah. It would be a damn sight better for the kids if they were indulged less and told the truth more.'

'You'd put them in work camps, I suppose, till they grew up and turned into adults who could discuss Big Issues.'

'That'd be better than sedating them with instant gratification. Aah, have a sweet, aah, you're right, aah, of course you need that pair of top-of-the-range trainers, of course you can dress like a slag when you're twelve, of course you can go on the competition trip and have your site on the web for perverts to drool over, of course you won because your essay was *so brilliant*, not because you're today's bait and when you turn twenty no one'll care what you think . . .'

'What'd *you* do?'

'Talk to them. Use reason. Make them *see* . . .'

'You're a child of the Enlightenment. I've news for you. They've turned the enlightenments off,' says Emma. At least she isn't shouting and crying now. 'They've never been trained to think. Or bothered to try.'

'It doesn't mean they can't.'

'So we parachute Socrates in for a crash course? And how many of us will be dead by then?'

'Dead?' I'm absolutely taken aback. She'd spoken calmly. I'd never known her exaggerate: that was my role in the relationship. 'We're not talking about death.'

'Of course not. Like the ickles aren't a potentially rioting, looting, stamping mob. Like Alice and Debs have humanistic values. Like we weren't talking about death with Galileo, and Salem, and the Stalin show-trials.'

'That's ridiculous. They're *kids*!'

She laughs first. After a few seconds, I join her.

Further down the beach, the goody-goods are watching us.

Chapter Ten

Rohini, 17, 5'2", black hair: I take an apology to the meeting. We'd worked and worked on it. Emma doesn't think it's enough. I think it's too much.

When we go down for supper, they welcome Emma and cold-shoulder me. They won't meet my eyes, they won't answer me. I end up eating alone, on the outskirts, until Emma stops talking to the goody-goods and comes to join me. Breadfruit, coconut and berries have never been so hard to eat. I'm once again amazed by how bleak it is to be excluded by people whose judgement I don't respect. I feel like an animal put out of the herd to die. I wonder about rephrasing the apology. Then I stop wondering, because 1) it's too late to re-write it, and they want it written, and 2) I'm being bullied. I won't be bullied into lying.

After supper Alice claps her hands and says the meeting'll be round the fire because it'll be dark in the clearing. She goes one side of the fire and all the others sit behind her, leaving me and Emma isolated opposite.

I read it out, holding the paper towards the fire so I can see. 'I want to say to you all that I'm sorry you've been frightened. I wouldn't want you to be frightened. I want us all to be as happy as we can, here on the island, till the rescuers come. I'm very sorry for any upset I've caused.'

I stop. They wait. Then Alice says blankly, 'That's it?'

'Yes,' I say.

'You haven't said what you did.'

'I did *nothing*.'

Debs says, in a saccharine voice, 'Did so, you kept the batteries.'

'I kept the batteries, yes, but –'

Tamsin points and howls. 'Liar! Liar!'

The ickles take it up. 'Liar! Liar! Liar!'

'Quiet,' says Alice. Her eyes pop as if she's swallowing a hard-boiled egg. I think she's aiming for dignified-but-appalled. It isn't funny, though. Insight: it isn't funny when you're by yourself. Neither is it the moment to exchange glances with Emma, even if she looks at me. 'We all just want to get this sorted out, Rohini,' says Alice, 'so we can all care and share.'

Nods from two of the goody-goods. 'Way to go,' says Debs.

For once in my life, I hold my tongue.

Alice waits for me to dig myself deeper.

I give her time to flounder.

The others are silent.

'We've gorra talk about this without you,' says Debs. 'Right, everyone? We've gorra talk about this . . . this situation, and with everyone's input . . .'

'With a co-operative discussion,' says Alice, 'cos we're all involved, we're all upset, it's been very upsetting and frightening . . .'

Pack murmurs and nods of agreement. Emma doesn't join in, of course, nor does Nadia, nor Tawheeda, nor one of the goody-goods, but all the others.

'Right, Rohini?' says Alice.

They're all waiting for me to go away. So I go.

I walk away from the firelight, up towards the baggage. I know if I give it time I'll be able to see well enough. There's some moonlight.

If it weren't for the bleakness I feel, it'd be beautiful. I can hear the big waves heaving the other side of the coral reef. I can see the stars, where the moon isn't. I wonder what they're doing at home now, and if they know already that I'm safe, and if the rescuers'll arrive any minute.

I'm coming up to the graves and can hear the rustly-rustle of the crabs, getting stuck in on the baby. I detour round them. No point in interfering with them now: I'd clear up early in the morning, just as I always did.

Self-pity creeping in.

'If you can't change the situation, change yourself,' I say. Out loud, in my quotation voice. It has about as much effect as pious exhortations usually do, namely none.

Failing a complete, instant restructuring of my personality, I'll *do* something. I go, carefully, feeling my way, to where I'd left the pills. There are horrid crackles and squishes each time I put my foot down once I get into the jungly bit. I resort to Nadia's song, slightly adapted: *Another bug bites the loam, squish. Another bug bites the loam, squash.* It's very dark now under the foliage. I use one of my reserve lighters to check the tree. The pills have gone.

I speak into the darkness. 'I know you're there somewhere,' I say. 'I can't imagine why you won't come out.' I wait. Nothing. No rustles, no movement. I speak louder this time. 'I know you're there. Come out to us. We'll look after you if you're ill: get you food, and things. It must be lonely by yourself. Come on out.'

No response. Earlier today, I bet I wouldn't have put the lonely bit in. I'd always assumed I liked being alone. This was a learning experience, for sure.

Emma, 17, 5'10", blonde hair: I couldn't leave the meeting until I was sure the worst was over, until something workable was agreed. I tried talking sense to Alice. Then I tried flattery. Since she was on this Miss Congeniality kick, I kept saying, I know you want to be fair . . . you won't want anyone to be unhappy, upset . . . I know you want to be fair. I kept saying fair until even Tamsin was sick of it.

The eventual deal was that we'd have a meeting in the morning. Alice would be fair. Rohini would share her feelings with us. Then, presumably, we'd share our feelings with her, then she'd share some more, and then we'd care, and then she'd care . . .

I plodded along the sand back to Rohini, carrying our sleeping-wraps. I knew she'd be in our rest-time place. I sat down beside her, gave her the wraps, told her about the arrangement. She made a noise like crying, and I hugged her, but actually she was laughing.

'What they actually want is a Communist self-criticism,' she said.

'Yeah, well,' I said.

'I've been thinking.'

'Surprise, surprise.'

'What're Alice and Debs behaving like?'

'Six horses' asses?'

'What kind of horse's ass? I'm serious.'

'The Misses Congeniality at a beauty pageant?'

'Close.'

'Enough with Socrates. I'm tired. Just tell me.'

'TV presenters. Game-show contestants. Oprah.'

I thought about it. Could be. 'Why would they do that?'

'They think this is a survival show. They think we're being watched.'

'Well, we probably are. By the man. I'm going to pee in deep jungle from now on, and wash under my towel.'

'Not by the man. By cameras. And listened to by microphones.'

'That's ridiculous . . . the island's far too big to cover . . . they'd never have taken the risk of the crash, and killing people . . . there'd have to be camera crews as well, they couldn't just leave them running . . . could they?'

'Of course it's ridiculous, but that doesn't mean they don't believe it. Alice certainly believes she's the most important person in the world, the galaxy, the universe, and *that's* ridiculous.'

'Come off it, Rohini, we *all* believe that. Otherwise we couldn't get up in the morning.'

'We *feel* it. We don't *believe* it.'

'Stuff semantics. I want to go to sleep.'

From the Man

I must join the girls now.

I will.

I'm profoundly depressed. I should have known that from the start.

I've been doing everything I can to jolt myself out of it. Reflex professional action, because, logically, being depressed is the ideal state of mind for suicide. Unless the suicide decision is purely the result of depression, but I won't accept that. If I accept it that removes the prospect of relief.

If I were treating myself I'd recommend in-patient care.

Lacking that option, I force myself to move about, to where the girls are, so I can track what's going on, force my brain to work, to tell them apart, to make judgements.

Most of the judgements I'm making are on myself, for the way we brought up my youngest daughter. Yes, she has a name (Cordelia), but to me she's always my youngest daughter. I have two others. By the time she was born I was in my forties, and successful. Successful enough to sit back and enjoy her. The hopes, discipline, pressures of my parenting went on the older ones. I let her mother spoil her and I spoiled her too, and she sounds, some of the time, like the worst of the younger children, the ones they call the ickles, the ones who've never stubbed their toes without an audience crying, '*Naughty chair!*'

Some of the older ones are probably fun, and talented. But the separation of age – not just now, ill, after the crash, but since I was about sixty – means I've lost the chance of knowing young girls. As friends. As equals. Certainly as lovers. Now, avuncularly, I can only enjoy their company in small doses. Enjoyment is usually enough to please them: they certainly expect it.

I refuse to be responsible for answers any more. I've been the Wizard of Oz twice, once as priest, once as psychologist, and the grinding emptiness of the machinery is swallowing me up. Nor will I be responsible for listening to people who say they want to be understood and only hear agreement and praise.

At the moment my patient on the island is me, and I'm at a loss. My usual pitch is hope, secular redemption, forgiveness, renewal, change, pathways forward. None of which is relevant, for me, here. Not in the cul-de-sac of death.

They're already protected by their adolescence, where everything is irrevocable and nothing is real.

It was thoughtful of the Indian to leave my pills, however.

Rohini, 17, 5'2", black hair: I get up at dawn to deal with the graves. The crabs have worked hard all night so I can work hard in the morning. I pile yesterday's dying flowers on top as tastefully as I can be bothered to, and go back to wake Emma up. She takes a while to come round but I'm not going to let her sleep on.

Eventually, since she has no choice, she gives in grumpily, sits up, says, 'What? What?'

'I spent most of last night thinking. No, listen. What we've got here is a political problem, OK? As in a democracy.'

'Alice's working more on a fascist/totalitarian model,' says Emma, and yawns.

'But she has to *pretend* she's democratic, right? No hierarchies?'

'Right, I spose. I don't see –'

'And what the ickles *really* want is to be told to do what they want to do already. They want to shift the responsibility.' (Ickle voice) "*We want GROWN-UPS. Where's the GROWN-UPS?*" All we've got to do is win hearts and minds.'

'Forget the minds,' she says.

'What they *think* are their minds, then. What they *feel*.'

'Bread and circuses?'

'That's the line Alice is taking, the competitions and memorial services and funerals and such. What we've got to do is give them a charismatic leader.'

'They've got one. It's Alice.'

'Uh-oh. A leader who they think'll take care of them. A leader they feel good about. Their dreams on two legs. Even the dopiest ickle's got to know in her heart of hearts that Alice is fakity-fake and stupidy-stupid.'

155

'It's not just the ickles,' Emma says. 'What about the older ones?'

'Aside from Alice and Debs? Nadia's a fully paid up member of the who-cares party. Rouchelle, Tawheeda and the goody-goods'll all go with who the ickles shout for, because aaah aaah, poor ickles. Plus, Vanessa's got a crush on Alice, and Alice'll have to go with the ickles.'

'So you'll be the leader,' she says, bored. She can't be bothered with ideas.

I don't click. Restraint. 'No. Our leaders is going to be *you*, Emma.'

'Uh-oh. No way. No way,' she says, delighted already.

'It's the *only* way, believe me. Think about it. You want the best for them.'

'Sort of,' she says.

'You do. Much more than Alice, you do. So, here's the campaign, you've got to do *exactly* what I say . . . stop yawning . . . listen . . .'

Anneka, 11, 5'1", mousy hair: Susan and I slept a little away from the fire last night, towards the baggage. Not as far as the graves, no way, but far enough to show we were sort of supporting Rohini and Emma, or that we weren't *not* supporting them, anyway. We didn't talk before we went to sleep. We usually do. Susan didn't even give me her goodnight whinny. The meeting had been really upsetting, and what they were doing to Rohini, who would never – I bet she hadn't – What if there is a man, anyway? He'd be nicer than most of this lot.

Emma got up much earlier than usual, cos she was

already at the fire when Susan and me got back from our morning wash and leaf tooth-clean. (Using leaves for your teeth was one of Rohini's good ideas. She has lots.) Emma was talking to Rouchelle and Tawheeda, being nice, saying how and it was everyone was so upset and how we'd all sort it out. Tawheeda was nodding and agreeing and then Rouchelle pointed and said, What's she doing?

I looked where she was pointing and it was Rohini standing on the coral reef right beside the tail of the plane, looking out to sea. She had a great pile of flowers beside her. She'd take one and throw it into the waves and then raise her arms. You could just hear that she was singing, the wind brought snatches of it, a weird song, like in the films you get from India on cable TV. She looked really lonely, all by herself, out by the sea.

It's a Hindu memorial ritual, said Emma, for the living and the dead, to ease their souls, for all of us.

Tawheeda said, I'll join her, say a prayer, if you don't think she'd mind a Christian.

Of course not, said Emma. She looked embarrassed.

Tawheeda went and Rouchelle followed her and then everyone started asking what was going on, and Susan said she wanted to get some flowers and do it for Megan and I helped her get some. By the time we were back on the beach people were saying how sad and lonely Rohini looked and the ickles were going for flowers and everyone was going out to the reef, Alice and Debs too. They were in front of us and they stopped before they got to the reef, quite a way before the reef, just standing in the lagoon. We had to go round them and I said, Aren't you coming? (I wouldn't of talked to them cept they've been really friendly recently) but Debs said, We're praying, piss off.

Debs, 16, 5'5", dyed blonde hair: Alice really gets on my tits sometimes. We really need to talk, but she's all for joining the Bollywood flower show. Rohini's up to something. Hindu memorial my bum. I can't make Alice see, she keeps on about clothes for the meeting and should she wear her hair up. Spoilt bitch, she doesn't know she's born.

Nadia, 14, 5'6", redhead: If only, if only I had paints. I got the Hindu memorial in pencil but I needed colour, colour, the flowers, the sea.

Then we had another meeting. Alice wanted to yak on about Rohini, I couldn't see why. Maybe Rohini doesn't want to admit it. Maybe she didn't do anything and there *is* a man. Who cares? He hasn't bothered us to date. Rosie said he was old. There's enough of us to sort him out if he makes trouble. More likely he's just buggered off when the going got rough, like my dad did.

The meeting was just a bit more interesting than last night's, mostly cos we didn't have so much of Alice. (Alice silent = to die for. Alice talking = shut ears.) Emma started off saying, This is a really important meeting so we've gotta have a chairperson, Tamsin would understand that. Tamsin said, Yeah sure you gotta have a chairperson, my mum says. Yeah, yeah, said the ickles. I vote Tamsin for the chairperson, said

Emma. Yeah, yeah, said the ickles. Alice smiled through her teeth, and I didn't like to think it because of Alice being . . . Alice, but she looked like the Big Bad Wolf.

Tamsin stood in the middle and Emma told her what to do, like suggestions. We could only speak one at a time and Tamsin had to decide who's to speak, and Emma asked to speak first, and Tamsin said yeah and Debs said Alice should speak first and Emma said it was up to Tamsin to decide, and Tamsin decided Emma.

She went and stood up on the rocks by the pool so she was higher than all of us and in one of the beams of light through the trees, so her hair shone.

She didn't talk about Rohini at all. She told us what she'd put in her competition essay, about women being the hope of the future and kinder and more sensitive than men and how we had to be nice, but being nice wasn't always easy, it was hard, but if we all cared for each other and stood together it wouldn't be so hard.

To do that it'd help to have a leader, and if she was our leader that's what she'd stand for, and it was hard work being a leader and a very important choice to make cos the leader would work out what we all really felt, like about the upset over Rohini, and consult everyone. She hoped they'd vote for her and give her a chance to do something good because she felt so sorry about the baby dying, and though she couldn't see what she did wrong with the baby and maybe it was just the baby's time to die, she felt bad about it and she wanted to do all she could for everyone else to sort of make up for it.

Then she sat down and said maybe Tamsin would

like to decide who'd speak next, and she did, and it was Alice, and she started on about Rohini and I stopped listening and just looked.

Then the leader thing was put to the vote and Emma won and she said the meeting had gone on long enough and we should get on with our lives, and Alice kept smiling, and I headed off to my bats.

Emma, 17, 5'10", blonde hair: After the meeting Nadia vanished, the goody-goods went off wood-collecting and fire-tending, Rouchelle and Tawheeda took Anneka and Susan to get food and the ickles went off to play. Rohini had already left, gone up to the baggage end. I was left with Alice and Debs. I felt very awkward. I knew they'd be angry, you could feel they were, but neither was showing it. They both congratulated me on being leader. Debs said, 'You're gonna tell us what you want us to do, right? Keep it going, keep everyone happy?'

I said I would. Then I said what Rohini had told me to, that we should have a party that evening before supper, and if Alice didn't mind I'd like her to organise it.

'We'll need stuff from the baggage,' said Alice.

'Of course,' I said.

'That'll be great,' sparkled Debs. 'We'll all have a great time!'

'Yeah!' said Alice. 'We got the message! Leave it to us!'

It should have been a relief to get back to Rohini, but as soon as I got close and saw her triumphant smile, I wanted to wipe it off her face.

'What did I tell you?' she said. 'Wasn't I right?'

'Clever-clogs,' I said. 'I feel awful. Awful.'

'Why?'

'About all of it. The ritual thing, Tawheeda believed in it −'

'They all believed in it, I hope −'

'But Tawheeda's a real Christian, and she asked me if you'd mind a Christian joining you, quite seriously. And her sincerity made me feel . . .' I couldn't find a word for it.

'Meretricious?' said Rohini. 'Meretricious is the point. They want meretricious, we give them meretricious. In spades. Flowers by the truckload. Multicultural mumbo-jumbo by the ton. Flattering words from here to Sydney.'

'I don't like it,' I said. 'We're being just as bad as Alice. She's jumping up and down for the cameras, we're jumping up and down for the others.'

Rohini sat down. 'Here,' she said, patting the sand beside her. 'I brought you a banana. I thought you'd be too excited to eat at breakfast.'

I sat down beside her, a little calmer, not much, and took the banana.

'Public speaking's very stressful,' she said. 'You did it well.'

'Did you think so? I meant most of it.'

'I know. It was your winning essay, wasn't it? The guts of your winning essay. You said it really well.'

'D'you think so?'

'I've just said it twice.' She was teasing.

'So in a way it wasn't dishonest. What I believe in is why I won.'

She rolled her eyes at me. 'Yeah . . . you could say that . . .'

'What else could you say?'

'How many telly ads did you do, in total, for Ken Wright and his merry media manipulators?'

'What's that got to do with it? Six, I think. Yes, six.'

'I did none. Nadia did two. Everyone else did one. Alice did three.'

'How d'you know?'

'The info was on the website.'

'So?'

'Why d'you think that was?'

'Don't know.'

'Did you notice the different sizes of the photos on our web pages?'

'Well, yeah . . . They tried to make me have mine bigger, but it looked stupid. Showing off. So I wouldn't let them.'

'They *did* make mine *smaller*.'

'So?'

Rohini sighed. 'How many hits in total did your web page have, before we left?'

'Don't know.'

'All of us had some hits. The ickles more than the older ones. The perv hit –'

'That's disgusting!'

Rohini clicked, impatiently, '– except for you, and Alice. Alice was in ten figures, and you were in the low trillions.'

'Hyperbole.'

'Of course, but the proportions are right.'

Silence. 'So the internet trawlers liked my essay?'

Rohini laughed. 'The kids elected you partly because you were the most familiar, and for the same reason that you had *become* the most familiar. Because you are tall, and blonde, and beautiful.'

'That's . . . ridiculous. That's . . .'

'And it didn't hurt that I stage-managed it,' said Rohini briskly. 'So don't go believing your publicity too much.'

'Of course not. But I'm pleased because at least now I can – not make up for the baby, exactly –'

Rohini clicked again. 'You did nothing *to* the baby. Debs gave you a *dead baby*. Stop this stupid female guilt.'

'Guilt's not just female.'

'It's not such a powerful bargaining tool with men.'

'Whatever. I still feel dreadful about it. But now I'm the leader I can really do it properly, and raise morale, and talk to them all, and comfort them, and encourage them to pass their time well. I can *do good*.'

'Call me Frankenstini,' said Rohini. 'I've created a monster.'

OK, she was joking, but it got up my nose all the same. I meant it about doing good, and I could. I could be nice. Really, really nice. Like in my essay. Really work hard, because it's difficult . . . I said, 'I didn't stress that in my speech, the bit about it being *difficult* not always to do what you want but to do what's best for other people –'

'It's often *difficult* for the people you're doing the best for, as well . . .'

She was being a real pain. 'Maybe I should have said it. I don't know why you told me not to.'

She clicked yet again. 'I told you to leave that bit out because it would've been a disaster if you put it in. Self-sacrifice? No way.'

'But it's the key issue I raise in the essay,' I said.

'So?' she said.

'You don't think much of my essay, do you?'

'I think your essay is an exploding supernova in the literary firmament, OK? I'll fax it right over to the Booker judges.'

I was narked, but I'd leave it, cos actually it wasn't *that* good . . . But it *had* won . . . 'Anyway, just because I didn't say it in the speech doesn't mean I can't *do* it. I can show them what I mean in what I do, and then maybe say it later.'

'Fine. Just don't expect them to be grateful.'

As if I would. She was arrogant and patronising. She was *really* annoying me now.

She was laughing. 'Just remember. All power corrupts. Absolute power —'

'Corrupts absolutely, and quoting gets you suffocated with a banana,' I said, and started to stuff it down her throat.

CHAPTER ELEVEN

Rohini, 17, 5'2", black hair: During rest-time today, I'm alone. The Newly Elected Leader, having spent the rest of the morning Moving Among Her People, isn't going to rest. Oh no. She decides to go and look at as much of the island as she can, parts we hadn't been to, in case there's anything useful or entertaining there. She asks me to come, but no chance. Getting up at dawn to clean up after the crabs doesn't exactly leave me feeling like Christopher Columbus after lunch.

I wait till she's well out of sight and then go back to the music tree, where I'd left the pills. I'd written a note to the man. Curiosity, I suppose. Also I really wanted to talk to another adult, even a possibly crazy one – though the more I live with this lot, the less crazy I think he is to want to avoid them.

I had several tries at the note. Finally I decided the simplest way to go was a playground dare. It ended up:

During rest-time, Tuesday

Dear Dr Montgomery
I would very much like to talk to you. I am

enclosing a pencil and paper with this, although I rather think you have some already. Write and let me know when would be convenient for you, and where.

You needn't be frightened.

Yours sincerely,

Rohini Sitaram

I prop it in the fork of the tree, whistle a few bars of Beethoven's Fifth, and go back to the baggage. This rest-time, I'd rest.

Alice, 18, 5'8", mid-brown hair with red highlights: Debs can be a major-league *drag*. I was all set to get some zzz at rest-time. We'd been getting the party sorted all morning. The kids make a noise like – like some kind of draggy high-pitched *noise*. I was getting one of my migraines that our doctor said aren't migraines, just headaches, so we changed our doctor. I could've got paracetamol but I didn't think of it till I was back at the clearing, and no way was I going all the way back to Rohini to ask, and the goody-goods were goody-gooding somewhere else, I couldn't ask Vanessa. I needed my kip, big-time.

But oh no oh no Debs drags me out to the lagoon for a *swim*. A *swim*. No consideration. Catch me getting my hair wet for a start, cos it's just about OK for the party and the hair thing is a real drag. No gloss, no mousse, no conditioner. And since the stupid kids had their stupid water-fight thing, not even *shampoo*. Water just doesn't do the job, it doesn't cut it. Debs said, We got some herbs here, shampoos are with herbs, you could use herbs. It didn't work. I need civilised herbs with all the badness taken out and all the goodness left in.

So she agreed no swim, we just sat in the shallow part looking to the cameras like we were enjoying nature. Then she started off at me. What to do about Emma?

I was angry about the Emma thing, first off, sure. But when I thought about it, it's not so bad. Everyone knows I'm the top one. They're scared of me. This leader thing, all it means is Emma gets to work all the time, and she gets the blame if something messes up. Sweet deal for me. Sharp work, cookie, Dads would say.

Debs didn't get it. She doesn't get it, more and more. I reckon it's her deprived background. She just kept saying, Rohini's *all right* now. We've *lost* Rohini. Lost Rohini what, I said. She's still here. Lost her as the bad one, Debs said. Why do we need a bad one? I said. To make you the good one, she said. But I *am* the good one, I said. No you're not, said Debs, and I took offence.

After long enough, I forgave her and said I'd talk about it if she wanted. Another problem, she said, Like, we've changed. What change, I said. She sighed, like she knows and I don't. She better watch it with me. I'll drop her like *that* if she gives me hassle. Before we sussed the cameras, she said, we were just, like, us. Now we're not us, I spose, I said. No we're not, we're, like, celebs, on camera the whole time, and if they're watching us now they must have been watching us before, so they'll have seen us not giving a toss, basically. Nothing wrong with that, I said, no one gives a toss *all* the time, it's not normal. Well we're gonna haveta get a cover story, that's all, why we've changed, she said.

You make it all confused, leave it simple, I said. I don't *make* it confused, it *is* confused, she said, I'll work on it. Can we go back now, I said. She said, Not yet, there's something else, we gorra widen our act, no way can I keep squealing happy-happy about the fucking parrots. I was the one thought of the parrots, I pointed out. We'd been stuck on the sunsets till then, plus you can't even see the sunsets, they're the other side of the island so the parrots are better. Yeah, yeah, so the parrots are better but they're not *enough*, she said. You're the one takes acting classes, whaddawe *do*?

Facer. The acting classes are great, sure, but they're not targeted at this particular situation. Tell you what – motivation, I said, we gotta get motivation! What's that, she said. It's, like, what you have inside, your reason for doing things, what you do things for, I said. That's easy, she said. It's money, that's what we're doing it for. That's not a motivation, I said. It is for me, she said. Not in acting class, I said. Can we go back in now? There's gorra be more tricks they teach you, she said, They've gorra tell you something, all those hours like teaching you, that your Dads pays for, what's he paying for, silence?

She's just jealous but I wasn't going to leave her thinking she'd put one over on me. You have to imagine, I said, like when there's a part you play, you have to imagine being that person, what they'd feel about . . . about . . . well, what they'd feel, and then if you imagine, you do. Do what? she said. Duh. Do what they'd do cos they feel it, I said. So you mean, like, I imagine I'm bright and bubbly and funny, she said. Yeah, I said, and nice, cos nice is hot right now. How do I imagine I'm nice? she said. No idea, I said, but I'm going back and getting my head down. *Now.*

Rohini, 17, 5'2", black hair: I thought he'd bite. Forget lonely, he must at least be bored. When I go back in the late afternoon, I get:

Later during rest-time, Tuesday

Dear Miss Sitaram,

Thank you for your note, for the pills and for the stationery supplies. You are correct in your assumption that I already have some but would be grateful for more.

I don't think it would be a good idea for us to meet. I am currently involved with an important task which I must complete without interruption.

I hope you are enjoying your stay on the island, though I imagine we both look forward to rescue.

Yours sincerely,
William Montgomery

He hadn't risen to the *frightened* bait. But he had risen to the communication bait. Ah ha, I thought, you're caught!

I won't describe the party. Enduring it was hard enough. The best I can say for it is that the batteries for the CD player lasted almost all through. Then after ten minutes' worth of the ickles singing (which Alice couldn't dance to: give her her due, she dances well) she says, Isn't it time for bed?

Never have she and I been in such perfect agreement.

Actually, I don't get to bed till much later. Emma and I collect the party clothes back, and the CDs, and as much of the jewellery as they'll relinquish. We set the baggage more or less to rights. Matching CDs to their cases will have to wait for daylight.

Then Emma and I have a ridiculous argument about where to sleep. We're up by the baggage, it isn't cold (it's never cold on this island – I'm beginning to miss cold) and it's a long way back to the fire.

'No, I really must . . .' she says.

'Really must what?'

'Really must be near the others. By the fire.'

'They'll all be asleep by now.'

'Still . . . they might –'

'Miss the glorious presence? Get real, Emma.'

'I'm tired. Don't bitch at me.'

'I'm tired, too.'

'You didn't hack round the island like I did. You had a rest.'

'Your choice.'

'I'm going back anyway.' She starts to walk and I follow her. What I want is to stay right there and go to sleep, Emma or not. But I know she'd take it as a slight and it would be a sign. So I follow her. Further on, one of us has to say something, but all I can think of is, Can we go to sleep here, please?

We're skirting the graves when she says, 'I can rely on you to sort out the graves tomorrow morning, as usual?'

'Yes, of course,' I say. Other responses come to mind, like: nothing is more designed to piss me off than your patronising co-option of the merit for a task which I (not you) saw needed doing and *have always done*.

She picks up my tone, tries to mollify me. 'Did I tell you I found another pool this afternoon?'

'Yes. Twice.' She's doing that self-important thing of talking so much to so many people that she forgets what she's said to a particular one. That habit doesn't usually set in till you're older in my experience. If we don't get off this island soon . . .

Nadia, 14, 5'6", redhead: Alice wore her Barbarian Queen kit again for the party, and I really wanted to draw her. She's much browner now. They all are, cept me and Anneka. Alice looks even more perfect, sort of fined down and dangerous. The way she puts her feet down, she's got high-arched feet, and at the party when she danced she flared and curled her toes, and slowly clsoed her eyes and looked sideways, like a cat, like a jungle cat, like her feet were alive. Every bit of her is alive and strong and she has lovely hands too.

Anneka, 11, 5'1", mousy hair: Since Emma was leader, it's been like I hoped this trip would be. Adventures and things to do and not being left out, being right in there, taking part. Not a big part, just a part. Last night I danced with the others, and sang at the end. I didn't know the tunes but that didn't matter. We all took turns doing special dances while we had CD music and I knew some of it cos it was from Granpa's time and he sings along when it's on the radio. Susan and I danced together and the others clapped.

The proper best dancers were Alice and Nadia. Alice's had lessons, she said, but I don't think it's just the lessons cos she moves like she's dancing anyway, that's why it's hard not to look at her even when she's sitting and sulking like a kid. I hated her before but now Emma's the leader Alice is OK, so I don't mind saying about the dancing thing. I've always liked Nadia so I'd have said about her being the best anyway. She looked amazing, too. She uzherly has her hair in a scruncher but she'd combed it out and it was like flames in the flames, and she seemed really happy, twirling and stamping and moving so it was like the music came through her and she was alive.

Which was odd, to me, thinking that, cos of course she was alive before. She smiles and makes jokes and teases the younger ones and helps the older ones. It's not that she's left out, but she doesn't have a special friend and it's like she's getting along because she has to, not cos she wants to. She never really talks, that I've seen, not like I talk to Susan, or Emma and Rohini talk to each other. All the other older ones do, they've all got someone.

Could be her age, she's fourteen, that's like in the middle. Maybe if someone else was fourteen. Maybe she talks to her drawings, that's all she needs, cept they can't talk back and that wouldn't be enough for me.

This morning Susan and me were collecting coconuts for Rouchelle and Tawheeda like we always do, and Emma came to find us. She's talking to everyone, on their own. She talked to Susan first and I kept climbing the trees and didn't listen, of course, but I could see Susan was crying a little and I spect she was talking about Megan, or maybe about Silver. Emma hugged her and Susan stopped crying and then it was my turn.

She began by saying what a good job I was doing, helping with food and wood and all. I said, yeah, pleased of course but blushing too, cos people saying nice things to me is really odd and upsetting, maybe cos I'm not used to it. Then she said, Is there anything you'd like to talk to me about.

People saying that (teachers frinstance) always shuts me right up. But this was Emma and I'd wanted to talk to her right from the start, and there were things I'd had in my mind that I hadn't said to even Susan. So I did. I said, Will they come and get us? She said yes of course they would.

Why haven't they come before?

I don't know, she said, but they will, you can count on it. She didn't look pleased with her answer, as if she wanted to give a proper one. I thought, maybe Rohini'd know, I should've asked Rohini. But I still wanted to talk to Emma, so I went on to the next thing.

It's about Tamsin, I said.

She nodded.

Tamsin says there's a book about kids like us on an island like this, and awful things happen. Like there's ghosts. And the ghosts make the kids kill each other. And Nadia says it isn't the ghosts that make the kids kill each other, it's what's inside the kids, cos they're bad inside. But Tamsin says anyway it won't happen to us, the book's about boys, and we're girls, so Tamsin says it's all right, we're girls, girls are *good* inside, which is why we got more rights –

I think – Emma started interrupting.

I went on anyway, cos if she said she wanted to listen she should listen, and it was muddled in my head and hard to say. I said, But my granpa says, there's something about girls, he always says.

I stopped then cos I didn't want her to say anything bad about Granpa, and I thought she might. Granpa isn't – not everyone thinks he's just ordinary, some people think he's, like, peculiar. They don't know about THAT BITCH (who used to be my granma till she left) and how she treated him, how she went off with THAT BASTARD (who used to be Granpa's best friend). That kind of thing could put you off women, it makes sense.

Your granpa's very important to you, isn't he, Emma said. Tell me what he says.

He says about girls, when they grow – like . . . I didn't want to say *tits* so I made a shape on my front with my hands . . . When they grow . . . they go mad. What does he mean?

Tell me about your granpa, she said. Do you live with him?

She hadn't answered the question. Maybe she didn't

know what he meant either. If so she should say so and not change the subject. But what d'you think he means? I said.

She sat there, looking as if she was thinking, and I hoped she was, not just making up something to shut me up with.

What d'you think he means? I said again.

I'm not sure. I could guess.

Guess, I said.

Some men think that women are too emotional, because their hormones influence them. You know about hormones?

Sure. Like the three friends did for the competition, PMS.

That's it. And when women have babies, while they're pregnant and just after, all their hormones are up and down. And looking after their babies, and even when the babies grow up and are quite old, women still feel really strongly about them, because of their hormones. And when women get older and stop having periods, their hormones go up and down again.

What do the hormones make them do?

Different things. They can make you angry or touchy or cry easily, or get things out of proportion.

I thought it over, then I said, You said, some *men* said that. Is it true?

Probly, she said.

So why don't women say it? I said.

She laughed. Some of them do, she said, maybe just not as much as men say it, and when women say it they also say, this means men should give special consideration to women, because they're upset, and they deserve to be treated carefully.

So Granpa's right, I said.

I don't think women go mad, she said. Not mad.

Just up and down and out of proportion, I said.

Well . . . yes, she said.

I said, Charlotte told me about the PMS thing. She said, some women have killed people when they have it, and then they haven't been punished, cos they weren't responsible. And Charlotte said it can be for four days or something, before your period. And nearly everybody on the island has periods. So that makes about twenty times four days which is eighty days in a month that –

She laughed. Don't worry about it, it's nothing like that, she said. Your granpa probably doesn't mean it anyhow.

I didn't say anything, cos I knew she was dead wrong. He did mean it.

After that she didn't ask me any more what *I* wanted to say, but told me about what *she* wanted to say, and I didn't have to listen to all of it cos it was just a pep talk like teachers give you, about being nice, like what she'd said at the leader meeting and probably what she was saying to everyone else. It sounded smooth, like she wasn't thinking about it, like she liked the sound of it.

So after she went away I went back to coconut-picking. I felt bad inside. When you look forward to something and it doesn't work the way you want it to, that's worse than if it hadn't happened at all.

She hadn't understood. Maybe no one ever does.

Even Susan doesn't acksherly listen to what I say, she waits till I've stopped talking then talks about what she wants to, which is fair I spose but disappointing too. Maybe that's what it's always like with friends and I wouldn't know, not having had a friend before.

Emma, 17, 5'10", blonde hair: I can tell all the ickles apart now and I know lots about each of them. It's taken three days, mostly because I've been very busy. We've had two good swimming sessions, on Wednesday and Thursday. (I'm picking up Rohini's sudden craze for giving the day of the week; she says it makes her feel closer to civilisation.) I helped them with their strokes and it was good fun.

I've talked to all the older ones too, and the same issues keep coming up. When will we be rescued, of course, and I've got nothing to say about that. Rohini says make something up if I must, if I can't bear not being the fount of all wisdom. That's bitchy, of course, but it's also wrong. There's pressure involved in being leader, the pressure of expectation. People look at you and want an answer, and you want to give it to them, to shape the world so it's safe for them.

Talking to people one by one, it's surprising how different they are. Debs, for instance. She's deeply upset about the baby, of course, but she absolutely didn't blame me. Her life's been extraordinarily hard. I had no idea.

Alice was actually friendly and encouraging. I think she's relieved not to have the responsibility and she's promised to think about another party for Saturday night (that's tomorrow). She said she'd think of something really special. Pity we're out of batteries, so no CD player. (Rohini just might have some more hidden, I'll ask her.)

A slight disappointment was not being able to get any of the goody-goods separately for our discussion. With the others, it just seemed to happen, but they're never apart. I wonder how healthy that is.

My one real failure's been Tamsin. At first she joined in with the swimming happily enough, but then every time I was paying attention to anyone but her, she'd get up to something, like pointing Susan in the wrong direction. That was nearly very unpleasant: Susan was swimming hard, straight for the open sea. Luckily Anneka noticed in time and brought her back. I spoke to Tamsin but she just made a face at me and then when I talked to her later I got nowhere. Now she doesn't join in any ickles activity when I'm there. She disappears, I've no idea where to.

I'd've asked Rohini, but she's been snappy and elusive for days. Could be some jealousy there.

Chapter Twelve

COLLECTED CORRESPONDENCE: Rohini
Sitaram and William Montgomery

Five o'clock, Tuesday

Dear Dr Montgomery,

I'm sorry you're too busy to meet me. I wonder
if you are the William Montgomery whose poems
were included in the anthology <u>British Poets
1950–1970</u>? I hope so, because as it was one of
my set books at A Level, I can claim at least a
surrogate acquaintance.

Perhaps you are now engaged in writing more
poetry? If so I should be most interested to see
it.

I wonder if you have seen two torches? They
seem to be missing from the cache. Also a bottle
– of whisky, I think.

I shall bring paper and pencils later today,
before the party if possible.

Yours sincerely,
Rohini Sitaram

★

During the party, Tuesday

Dear Miss Sitaram,

Once again I must thank you, this time for the pens and pencils.

I am the author of some poems in the collection you mention. That I was included is a reflection on the standard of British poetry, 1950–1970. I trust you did well in the examination.

I have indeed taken the torches and the whisky.

It would be considerate on your part not to reply to this letter. I would prefer to be left alone.

Yours sincerely,
    William Montgomery

★

Not long after dawn, Wednesday

Dear Dr Montgomery,

I think you are very rude, and I'm concerned for your mental health.

Yours sincerely,
    Rohini Sitaram

★

Mid-morning, Wednesday

Dear Miss Sitaram,

You are right on both counts.
    Yours sincerely,
        William Montgomery

★

During rest-time, Wednesday

Dear Dr Montgomery,

Perhaps you should have some consideration for me: you have purloined the only readable books on the island; your appropriation of the CD player and use of the batteries has precluded me from the enjoyment of music; your voluntary sequestration confines me to the company of my peers.
    More than this, surely you should consider yourself as being, in some senses if not all, responsible for a group so much younger than you?
    Yours sincerely,
        Rohini Sitaram

★

During your supper, Wednesday

Dear Miss S,

I am keeping a close eye on the group. It is functioning very well without me.
    Your prose style seems to be lurching uneasily towards Henry James. Why? W.M.

★

181

Just after dawn, Thursday

Dear Dr M,

Perhaps because I am still in search of a style, as you were, 1950–1970.

The group may be functioning well, but <u>I am not</u>. R.S.

★

Mid-morning, Thursday

Dear Miss R,

<u>Yes you are</u>. WM

★

During rest-time, Thursday

Dear Dr M,

This morning I waited by the pool you use for water. I then followed you back to your tree, waited till you left again, and read what you had written about yourself and about our group. I have also repossessed the copy of <u>Swann's Way</u>.

If you do not agree to meet me, I shall tell the others where you are. R.S.

★

During your supper, Thursday: R.S., has no one ever told you it is absolutely unacceptable to read private papers? W.M.

After supper, Thursday: WM: Yes they have. The same sort of people who thought it acceptable to steal my country, India. RS

Early hours, Friday: RS, You are no more Indian than I am. WM

Just after dawn, Friday: WM: unless I meet you, how can I tell? RS
    P.S. Meet me, or I drop you in it. Last warning.

Mid-morning, Friday: RS: I will meet you during what you call rest-time, today, at my pool. WM

★

Rohini, 17, 5'2", black hair: His pool's more hidden than ours, it doesn't have a clearing round it, just over-arching trees, jostling. The water drops down to it in a series of little falls, like an elaborate water-feature. When it gets to ground level it broadens out into a rock-pool about two metres in diameter, much smaller than ours. The trees are so thick round it that all the light's green, like being underwater. He's sitting on a rock beside one of the little waterfalls, face tilted back to the spray. He's wearing a tattered pair of chinos, a sweatshirt and trainers.

I'd expected him to be old and sick. He looks old, but normal old, not old-person old. He's middle-size and middle-weight and what hair he has is grey-white, cut very short. He might have been attractive, once. You wouldn't, looking at him, immediately expect him to be senile or incontinent or particularly deserving of consideration. He doesn't look sick at all.

'You let the baby die,' I say, surprising myself. I hadn't known that was in the forefront of my mind.

'I know nothing at all about babies,' he says.

'You've got at least four children.'

'Quite. I repeat, I know nothing at all about babies. If I'd have had a relevant suggestion, I'd have made it.'

'But you're a doctor.'

'Not that sort of doctor. You were ill-advised to force this meeting, you know.'

I'm left with a smile which had started as welcoming and slightly triumphant, but which hangs on as foolish. 'I was worried about you,' I say.

'Commendable. Or impertinent.'

'I didn't mean to be impertinent.'

'No, probably not. Pert, perhaps.'

'Not just,' I say, baffled by the effectiveness of his keeping-off shield. 'You are interested in us. You must be. Otherwise you wouldn't have written about us.'

'Ever heard about counting sheep in order to sleep?'

'Of course.'

'Does it require an interest in sheep?'

'You're getting very wet. The spray.'

'Then I stand in the sun until it dries me.'

'We've been lucky with the weather,' I say, before realising what a stupid remark it is.

'Do you want to tell me about yourself?' he says.

'Not in the least. You're obsessed with that. Over-work, I expect, bound to happen in a psychologist.

Are you the lie-on-a-couch-talk-about-your-mother sort?'

'Not a Freudian. No couch. Not necessarily your mother. Otherwise, spot on.'

'And what did you mean about being the Wizard of Oz?' He ignores that. 'I was hoping for a discussion of general interest,' I say.

He laughs, a sort of growly bark. 'Fine. Start one.'

'I've been trying to work out why we haven't been rescued yet. I haven't come up with an answer. Can you?'

He moves from his rock, slowly, carefully, picks his way down to ground level, leans against a tree. Moving makes him look vulnerable, as if he's afraid he'd fall. He's physically closer to me now but he's leaning with folded arms, very enclosed, shutting me out.

'Technology's not my line,' he says.

'Won't you even tell me your ideas?'

'They'll be primitive.'

'They can't be more primitive than mine.'

'I'm going along the line of inferior equipment and maintenance. Wright's is a cut-rate airline. Everything he does is shoddy. If the electronics on the plane went down, the pilots may not have known where they were, in the storm. So the information they gave may have been wrong, and the search may have started in the wrong place. The South Pacific's huge.'

'And the black box thing that's supposed to guide people to the plane?'

'Also badly maintained.'

'So you think they will come?' I sound more plaintive than I'd meant to.

'Of course they will,' he says. Then looks annoyed, as if he's being more reassuring than he meant to. I feel sorry, as if I've tricked him into an involvement he'd said from the beginning he didn't want. I feel sorry altogether, that perhaps I'd treated him as a part of my life when he wanted to be left squarely in his own, bleak as that was. In person he's much more coherent and more considerable than he'd seemed in writing. I'd actually thought he needed looking after. Either he's recovered and he doesn't any more, or he's good at hiding it. Or − most uncomfortable of all − perhaps he does, but nobody can.

'Are you all right for clothes?'

'Thank you, yes. I've taken what I need.'

He's waiting for me to go. 'Thanks for meeting me.'

'I hardly had much choice,' he says. 'Goodbye.'

I want . . . I don't know what I want, though, uneasily, I think that he thinks he knows what I want, and he isn't going to give it to me.

I had to try. 'I just need a break,' I say. 'From the women. It's all so *petty*. Does she think and did she say and is she offended and didn't I smile enough and what do I feel and how am I now and would I feel better if I . . . like taking a temperature *all the time* until the patient dies of a ruptured throat.'

'Or, in France, of a ruptured bowel,' he says.

Was that irrational? Was it a sophisticated joke? I'm floundering, which he sees.

'In France they take rectal temperatures,' he says.

'Oh,' I say, and smile. It's too late to laugh. 'But do you see what I mean about petty?'

'I think petty is a name we give to interests we don't share,' he says.

Which is a snub, and a psychologist's cheat.

'Goodbye,' I say, and leave him there.

The way back to the beach from his pool is hard enough to find at the best of times. It isn't made any easier by tears. I'm annoyed with myself for crying. It's that general sort of crying, usually prompted by something minor, which ends up, if you're not careful, in a lament for the world, the universe and everything. I don't let myself indulge it.

Back at the beach I collapse gratefully into lamenting's cure, a heartfelt bitch at something else. In this case it's Emma. She's sitting along towards the fire, heart-to-hearting with an ickle. I'm glad she's not up here otherwise I'd have to talk to her, I think, and her brain's gone soft. When my cousin Kavita had her first baby, suddenly she lost her grip on reality totally, and what the baby looked like and ate and defecated became all there was. But at least Kavita *had* a baby. There was a baby present (too often for my liking). Emma's baby-equivalent is this stupid idea she has of herself as carer, herself as leader. She's so wrapped up in it that it's gone into some serious, sacred zone you can't joke about. I hate it when there are things you can't joke about, or if you do, you get a bland, forgiving smile.

After which explosion of malice I stop crying and feel quite well-disposed towards Emma. Enough to wave her towards me when she leaves the ickle with a concluding hug.

From the Man

The irony is, I actually feel better today than I have felt for months. Probably a purely physical improvement – a very simple life, led by force, a simple diet, plenty of exercise, no alcohol, no real stress. I feel so much better that I don't want to die any more.

Also, now I'm strong enough, I can think about the event that all my (flat, dull) attempts to become an island were probably an attempt to avoid, were certainly (be honest) an attempt to avoid. The fact that my second wife has left me.

A reader of this would have worked that out already, I think. My not referring to her by name. Now I'll say her name. Helen. Helen has left me. She left me just weeks before I decided to take my trip to Ayers Rock.

Wives always leave when you least expect it. My first wife did, too. There'd been plenty of times in my marriage with Helen when I would not have been surprised to find her gone. Terrible, struggling, turbulent times. Or dull, grinding, resentful times. And plenty of times that I'd have been relieved if she had. But not just then, not when she did. I'd thought the marriage was under control, that we'd reached an exhausted peace. Perhaps from her point of view an exhausted peace was just what she couldn't endure. Not an exhausted peace leading to an exhausted old age.

I now understand the crushing selfishness of depression from the inside. All these years, I knew the theory, I had sympathy for my patients and, I thought, understanding. Underneath it all, though, I had what I now see is the healthy man's contempt for the sick. Underlying it was a belief that if only the patient would try, he could pull himself together. Buried deep deep deep, under layers of training, knowing that was exactly what I should not believe, because it wasn't true. It was instinctive, I think, a form of self-preservation.

Here I was on the island and absolutely nothing caught my attention apart from my own misery. The outside was switched off. No input at all. Not the sights of it or the sounds. Not the girls. I forced myself to tell them apart and had to label them by height and age and hair colour, and even so they slipped away from me, because there were only two people in my world: Me (miserable) and Them (not miserable, not important).

Now I feel better, I can see. It's as simple as a focus-twist on a camera. And already I'm beginning to find rationalisations which quite soon will leave me not having been depressed at all, because remembering the fact is remembering the pain.

A physical cure has led to a mental remission: I won't be foolishly optimistic and say cure. It is just feelings, that is all it is, nothing to do with thoughts. All my thinking couldn't help me.

While my feelings last, I'll enjoy it. Perhaps, when

I watch the girls and listen to them now, I'll take more of it in.

Already I feel a stirring of professional interest. I'm concerned for Charlotte. You may well not remember who Charlotte is, which is a pointer to my concern. Charlotte is one of the group they call the goody-goods – the one who is neither Vanessa nor Mei Lin. She's often signalled her wish to escape from the three-some. She's never the one to link arms, always the linkee. She disagrees with them on minor issues, and on major ones: she is not nearly so enamoured of Alice as Vanessa is.

When she goes into the jungle to pee, there's almost always a minor skirmish, as follows:

Vanessa: I'll come with you.
Charlotte: No, no that's fine.
Mei Lin: We'll both come with you.
Charlotte: No, no, that's fine, really.
Vanessa: We don't mind at all, do we, Mei-Mei?
Mei Lin: Of course not, we'll come with you.
Charlotte: But . . .
Vanessa: Don't be silly, we don't mind.

Charlotte always loses the battle, but it would be a mistake for the other two to think that the war will be easily won.

I wonder how professional my sympathy is, now I re-read what I've written. This blanketing mothering co-opting process was my complaint against Helen. She was never satisfied by what I was prepared to give. She always wanted more. She was a bottomless pit into which she demanded that I pour endless personal tedious information. Bulletins on my movements, my feelings, my dreams. Requests to accompany her while she performed tasks she could perform perfectly well without me.

Her version would be different, of course.

Emma, 17, 5'10", blonde hair: Rohini waved to me and I felt a great surge of relief. She'd been so shut off ever since I got to be leader. She hasn't met my eye, not properly, she hasn't fully smiled at me. I found reasons at first for why it wasn't happening, and then why it didn't matter, but all of that was lies, to myself. It was happening and it did matter and maybe now it would stop.

I went up to her, beside the baggage, and we sat down together just as we had for the first week, and started making leaf-hats. (She'd kept making them for the last few days.)

We felt awkward together in the hat-making silence, the first time I could remember that we had. I said the first thing that came into my head. 'What d'you suppose is in the *right woman!* theme park? If we ever get there?'

'The what?' she said.

'Part of our prize. In Australia. Ken Wright's theme park.'

'Would you believe I'd forgotten it?'

'Surprise me. Surely it's the subject of your every waking thought.'

We smiled. The situation was bedding down. It was her turn.

'OK. The theme park. There'll be lots of merchandise. And some kind of laser show, with skimpily dressed great women through the ages, culminating in Lara Croft.'

Pause while we both contemplated this.

'He'll be scraping the barrel,' she went on.

'Why? Plenty of great women,' I said.

'Very few.'

'They haven't had the chances.'

'Now they have the chances, are they popping up like beetles?'

'That's maybe because men define what's great,' I said.

'Of course if you define as great what women are good at, you'll get more great women,' she said.

Both of us were carrying on the conversation with a fraction of our attention. 'I need your help,' I said.

'If I can,' she said.

'I don't know what else to do,' I said. 'What they really want is to get off the island. I can't do that for them. Everything else is just pretence.'

'Ah,' she said. 'Anthropologically speaking, that's where religions come from, don't you think?'

'What?'

'The answer to the problem of death. Powerlessness against death.'

I was utterly at sea and if we'd been fully back to our friendship I'd've said so. As it was, I nodded, and tried to work out what she meant.

She went on, 'Like medicine men. That's what you've been doing, a medicine-man thing, going round laying on hands, reassuring them, affirming them.'

'How do you know?'

'Because in this situation, that's all you could do,' she said. 'You can't tell them when the rescuers are coming, because you don't know.' Silence. 'It's to do with politics as well,' she said. 'It's to do with everything.'

I was still floundering, but I knew I was. I couldn't work out her meaning, and there was no point in not admitting it. She might understand what was going on, and it was time to let go any jealousy. Or indeed my (smug, I admitted to myself) belief that I had some magic power. I had felt it as that. Just me had brought them something. Or maybe I had only thought it had. 'You jump, I don't,' I said. 'Give me the bits you're leaving out.' That was the formula I used with Christie, had used ever since we were small. It didn't always mean I managed to follow her in the end, but at least it gave me a sporting chance.

'OK. Point one, we're in an artificial situation here. All our thoughts are bent in one direction, when will we be rescued. We're waiting for that.'

'Right,' I said.

'That makes it simpler for all of us in one way. Whatever it is we look forward to and hope for when we're off the island and leading our normal lives, we've put that aside. All the richness of things that makes us different doesn't really exist here. It's down to one thing. Like people being happier in wartime.'

'Happier?'

'Depends how you define happy. Obviously not at the moment you're killed, or in battle, or when dreadful things are happening to you or your family. But overall, as a group, you're looking forward to victory, and working against the enemy.'

'So you're saying we should be happy here? But we're not.'

'That's because we don't have an enemy. That's why I bet it was a relief to all of them when they sat the other side of the fire, hating me. They knew whose fault it was.'

'And whose fault *is* it?' I said.

'You mean why we crashed? Probably, practically, Ken Wright's. But more generally, no one's of course. It's the human condition. Why don't I get the man I want, the job I want? Why illness? Why pain? Why death? Just *because*.'

I thought about it until my brain hurt, or maybe it was my feelings that hurt. 'But what should I *do*?' I said. 'For the rest of them. I'm supposed to be leader. I'm supposed to look after them.'

'There've been lots of answers to that.'

'Run them by me.'

'Life after death, rewards, you're losing here, you'll win there; clock up the supermarket tokens, do the rituals, deny yourself, die for your faith. The personal enemy: it's all because of a named so-and-so of the time like Hitler or Nixon or Thatcher or Hussein or bin Laden or Dad or the devil. Or a group enemy: whites, blacks, yellows, Jews, smokers, drinkers, men, women, gays, asylum seekers stroke illegal immigrants, drug addicts, welfare scroungers, single mothers, the young, the middle-aged, the old, the media, paedophiles. The ideological enemy: it's all because of Hinduism, Christianity, Judaism, Islam, capitalism, communism, left-wingers, right-wingers, colonialists. Single-issue enemies: it's all because of video games, rap music, the decline of Latin, capital punishment, fox-hunting, guns, cars, Big Government, environmental polluters, class structures, globalisation —'

'Stop a minute,' I said. 'Stop.' The flood of words breaking over me took me to a place I didn't want to go, a place I knew too well, because Christie spent a lot of her time there. When Christie talked like this it made me feel left out. Not because I couldn't follow her (though sometimes I couldn't), but because she cared more about the ideas than she did about me. She was moving to a place where people didn't matter, the argument did. Rick did it sometimes too.

Rohini stopped. She looked deeply disappointed, then she caught herself, and put back the usual face. 'Sorry,' she said. 'I forgot the question.'

'The question is, what do I do? For the best.'

'OK. Well, your basic problem is giving them something to do, and something to look forward to. The somethigns-to-do must be short-term, achievable, and take some effort.'

'Why?'

'To fill up the time and make them pleased about themselves. Your problem with that is what they've been trained to do.'

'Which is what?'

'It varies. But I suppose you mean the ickles, mostly?'

'Mostly.'

'They've been trained to *do* nothing, just to be, to feel, and to consume.'

'You're not really helping,' I said. I said it nicely but she picked up the irritation underneath.

'Sorry,' she said. She sounded disappointed.

I tried to think of a general issue of my own to offer her as a sop. 'It makes it easier that there aren't any boys here, anyway.'

'Makes it easier how?'

'We don't have the problem of sex.'

'I don't think sex, as in having sex with men, is often an issue with women anyway,' she said.

Her tone was purposely non-confrontational and I tried to go along. My instinctive response was, How would *you* know? But that was bitchy and probably stupid as well.

'That's too complicated for me,' I said. 'My point is just, we haven't any boys to fight over here.'

'True,' she said.

I thought she was going to go on, but she didn't. I didn't want the conversation to stop there, at cross-purposes. 'Give me a suggestion,' I said. 'Give me a practical suggestion. Just one, briefly.'

She smiled. 'Can I make it three, pretty please?'

'OK. Three.'

'Number one, remember you must die.'

'Like the slave whispering beside the Roman Emperor, to remind him not to get above himself?'

'Exactly. Number two, don't expect consistency from your subjects. Any of them.'

'OK. And number three?'

'Find out what Tamsin's up to.'

Debs, 16, 5'5", dyed blonde hair: Alice says Marbella's posher than Torremolinos so that's where my villa's goin to be, and I've decided, chin first, then tits, or maybe as they're not exactly close they could both be done at the same op. I've got the *nice* act smooth. Brilliant. Better than Alice. She doesn't get it about how you've gorra keep topping up the material, so what you do isn't say the same thing all the time, but, like, take what's there. Frinstance if one of the goody-goods needs help with the fire, then you help her, and talk about what you're doing, or if one of the ickles wants someone to watch her, then you watch her and talk about what she's doing. Or ask any of them about themselves, that's a good one.

And the payoff's better than you'd think. Fighting all the time – like I always did cos you'd gotta fight your corner or else they'd rip you off – it's what you've gorra do, I knew that from a kid, it's the right thing to do but it's hard work, like going uphill all the time. I never knew that. I mean I knew every-thing was hard work like looking after the kids and Mum, I knew that was extra hard work that *I'd* gorra do, but fighting your corner, I thought that was what *everyone* did. But if you don't do it, like me now cos that isn't part of the act, then life's like *easy*.

The muscles in my neck, I never noticed them before cos they was always knotted up, but now they've kinda gone soft and they don't hurt. And I look good with my tan.

Tamsin's in a snit, been in a snit for days. I keep away from her cos all she does is bitch and whine, and New Sparky Debs doesn't work with her. Either I agree with her, so I'm a bitch, or I tell her she's talking crap, so I'm a bitch. Lose-lose. Rohini's u/s too, she sort of messes round with words, leaves you with egg on your face. She's not buying the act.

'Sgood all round that I sussed the cameras cos otherwise I'd haveta do something with Alice, and tell the truth she's not easy. If it was just us on the island she'd be sulking 24/7 and I'd be running round getting things for her and keeping her important, and nothing's ever enough for Alice. As it is I get away from her lots and, like, make my own mark, cept when we're setting up functions, like the party tomorrow night. Party's gonna be hard to do, no proper music, gotta stop the ickles singing too much. We're gonna have talent acts, like everyone's gotta do something, spread the load a bit.

Saturday night, tomorrow night is. Two weeks since the crash. It's not been all bad, no way. Cept the baby, poor little sod. I like sleeping out by the fire, looking at the sky, like now. Alice snores, that's funny, she doesn't know it. Could be irritating but I don't mind cos it's funny she doesn't know, and we've got the best place to sleep, and it's kind of familiar.

I think I'll call my villa 'Debs'. She says her dad's gorra sailing boat called *Alice*. I might get a sailing boat as well. If I end up liking sailing, which I've never tried.

CHAPTER THIRTEEN

Anneka, 11, 5'1", mousy hair: It's Saturday morning, Emma told me. Saturday morning. I'd forgotten days of the week. It's like time goes without cutting it up here, maybe cos we're just waiting. Saying Saturday makes me think of home.

Susan and me's got plans. For when we get back. She's going to ask me to stay at her house, so I can meet Silver, and maybe learn to ride. She says it takes ages to learn to ride but I think maybe she's just saying that, cos how hard can it be, to sit on top of a horse? There's things to put your feet into and hold on to, and I reckon I could do it really quick. Granpa says I'm well co-ordinated.

I said I'd ask her back but it won't happen cos I don't have a house or a family like her, but we kind of both knew that, and it didn't matter. She's a real friend.

Tamsin played a trick on her, first thing. Susan was washing and Tamsin took her clothes and put others there. Susan put them on and they were much too big, and she was upset, and then Alice came and said they were hers and took them, which left Susan with no clothes. Alice was smiling and laughing about it but she didn't have to take them, she's got three sets, and me and Susan had to go up to the baggage with Rohini and get more, and all the way up the beach Susan had just her pants and bra on and the rest of the kids were silly.

Tamsin's off somewhere else now. She's always going off by herself, the last few days. And getting up early. She used to be still asleep when I woke up, and even still asleep when most of us were having breakfast. Now when I wake up she's gone. Which is why she got Susan's clothes, cos I wasn't keeping my eye on her, cos I couldn't, cos she'd gone.

When Susan got her clothes back we went wood-clecting with the three friends. Debs came too. It was good fun. We were all talking bout what we'd do for our talent spot for the party tonight, we'd none of us made up our minds, Susan speshly. She's shy. Debs said whatever we did it would be great.

Then we were talking about telly and the ads we did, and Susan was saying about how it'd been all right for her cos they wanted her riding Silver so she thought about Silver and not about her at all, and she almost enjoyed it. Then Charlotte talked most, she hardly ever does, about her father who's a telly producer and how she'd been disappointed when he told her how it all worked. Like when they said someone was alone like on an island like this and they had to survive by themselves, and would they find water, Charlotte said of course they'd have water cos there was always the camera crew there and they'd need water, no one was ever alone, there was always a camera crew. Unless they were filming themselves, and most people couldn't.

Debs was really interested and said couldn't they leave the cameras running? And Charlotte explained why they couldn't and I didn't listen to that bit cos I was picking up the wood Debs was dropping, she really wasn't concentrating.

Then after that Debs went away and I thought she was crying but she said she'd got a bug in her eye so I didn't push it, and then we'd got enough wood so Susan and me went to help Rouchelle and Tawheeda clect the food, cos I thought, keep Susan away from the other kids, speshly Tamsin, just at the minute.

Alice, 18, 5'8", mid-brown hair with red highlights: Debs's lost it. She shouted at me, well out of order, I won't have that. I said, I won't have that, uh-oh, no way, you've gotta treat me with respect. I was trying to make plans for the party, that's the most important thing right now. I was sitting on a rock up above the pool, good pose, looking, like, thoughtful.

She went on and on about no cameras, no cameras, and her voice was wrong, bitchy and screamy. I kept *my* voice right, understanding voice. I didn't know what she was on about but I didn't let on. Then she went away and I went on doing thoughtful look, plus I'd added concerned-for-Debs look. I had to shift just a bit cos I was getting cramp in my leg.

William Montgomery, 70, 5'10", grey hair: This morning's sunrise was stunning. I'd slept high up, near the skull shrine (interesting) and I woke bathed in light to the cries of the can't can't bird. I felt less stiff than I usually did in the morning. Not sleeping in trees is paying off, and high up I'm perfectly safe from the girls. At night they never leave the fireside, let alone the beach.

I'd already decided that today was the day I'd join the group, so after I'd had a wash I intended to leave a note for Rohini in what she calls the music tree. Better for her to introduce me to the others, I thought. I'd find her alone and talk to her if I could, failing that I'd draw her attention to the note somehow.

But when I went to what I think of as my home tree for writing materials, I found someone had plundered my things. There was just enough left to write with, scattered about, but the whisky had gone, as had all the writing I'd done. It was purposeful theft, a child not an animal.

My first reaction was annoyance. I profoundly dislike any interference with my private things. My second was concern: they might be frightened. Now they will certainly know that there is someone else here, the Rohini — trick fiction they've decided on will no longer do, and stepping out unheralded would be even more frightening for them. So I went ahead with my note to Rohini, including information about the theft, and reinstalled myself high up in the music tree, awaiting an opportunity.

Debs, 16, 5'5", dyed blonde hair: She's so fuckin stupid. So fuckin stupid. There's no way to say how fuckin *stupid* she is.

I've been fuckin stupid 'swell, to believe any of it

would happen. It happens, right, to other people, but not to me. There'll always be boats called *Alice*. There'll never be boats called *Debs*.

Now I can do what I want. I don't haveta put it on. I can be just me.

I don't know, right now this minute, what just me'll do.

I gotta stop crying. I do stop. Then I start again. So I go to find an empty place, bit up the path, away.

Sod it, no place is empty when you want it empty. Near the path the branches are moving, like someone's just gone through and they're swinging back to cover it, but not quick enough. Who is it, I say. C'mere.

'Sme, says Tamsin, sticking her head out. She's got something she doesn't want me to see so I grab her hands. OK, OK, leggo, she says, you're hurting me, and I take what she's got. It's the rape alarm thing that Rohini never leaves go of, and her bothering to have it's a joke. Who'd rape her?

How'd you get it? I says.

That's for me to know and you to find out, she says, and I belt her cross the legs. How'd you get it? I says, still holding on to her.

She snivels but not for long. She's OK, Tamsin, got guts. I gorrit from her shorts when she washed, she says.

I take it, put it in my pocket. Mine now. I'm still holding on to her. Leggo, that hurts, she says. I reckon she'll be on about her rights any minute. Shurrup, I says, an one word bout your fuckin rights an I'll belt you cross the face.

She shuts up.

203

Now show me what else you got, I says.

What d'ya mean what else, she says.

I twist her arm. OK, she says, leggo, I'll show you.

I don't leggo till she shows me.

Emma, 17, 5'10", blonde: I don't know where Rohini's gone this morning. I saw her at breakfast, we didn't speak because I was discussing plans for the party with Alice, and then afterwards she'd disappeared. She wasn't up by the baggage, I could see. I noticed it without worrying about it and got on with a swimming lesson for the ickles. But when it was getting on for lunchtime I really needed to find her. Alice was hoping there'd be some batteries left for the CD player for the party and only Rohini knew about our stocks. Maybe, I thought, she should share all her information with me. It didn't look good, me being leader and not knowing. I'd mention it when I saw her.

But I didn't see her.

I was looking in the jungle behind the baggage when I heard the rape alarm. Good, I thought, that's where she'll be.

I walked up to the clearing, where the sound had come from. It had scared the birds, it always did. The parrots were circling the clearing making their usual din and the can't can't bird called. I liked its sound. Maybe one day I'd see it.

The rape alarm kept going off, annoyingly, like someone going on and on at a doorbell. I was the last to the clearing, just a few ickles ahead of me, because I'd been furthest away. To be honest I was a bit annoyed that Rohini had called a meeting without

204

consulting me first, but when I was in the clearing I stopped short.

It wasn't Rohini with the rape alarm. It was Debs.

I walked straight up to her but she ignored me and went to stand up on the rocks, on the place Rohini had told me to make my leader speech from. I followed her but she went right on ignoring me and shouted over my head.

'Shurrup . . . Shurrup . . . sit down quick, you lot, listen.'

They all did, and I did too. They were frightened by her tone. I almost was. It was like the old Debs, but more so. Almost vicious.

And Rohini wasn't there. Neither was Nadia.

Debs went right on. 'I know things you don't know, I found out things. Terrible things. SHURRUP!'

The ickles were silent. Rouchelle and Tawheeda whispered to each other.

'There's a man on this island and we gorra find him. Now.' She looked at me. I blushed, I didn't know why. 'Emma's been lying to you,' she said. 'She's been lying to you.'

'What's going on?' said Alice. She was sitting by herself, on one of the other rocks.

'Shurrup,' said Debs, straight at Alice, and Alice gasped.

Debs went right on. 'We've gorra find the man, now, and then I'll tell you all what's been going on. Terrible things. Scary things. First we gorra find the man.'

I didn't know what to say. Of course there was a man, but I'd put him to the back of my mind. He wasn't bothering us, we wouldn't bother him. But I didn't want to say I knew there was one because somehow Debs was knitting his presence into whatever she was on about, and it would've looked like an admission.

'So what we're going to do, we're going to space ourselves out along the other end of the beach, and then we're going to go inwards, keeping a space between us, and we're going to search. And how we're going to search, we're going to look up. Cos he lives in a tree. And when you find him, shout out.'

The ickles were still silent. I didn't blame them. Debs was scaring me. It was particularly shocking after how nice she'd been the last few days. Her tone was vicious. Vicious, and malevolent. Obviously I had to look cool, not to scare the younger ones myself, and it'd look bad if they thought I was losing it. I had to clear my throat twice before I could speak. 'Where's Rohini?' I said. 'Why've you got her rape alarm?'

'Don't worry about that now,' she said. 'We've gorra find the man. Get that, everyone? GEDDIT?'

'I don't – began Alice.

'GEDDIT?' said Debs.

Yes, yes, the ickles said.

I said, 'Of course, Debs, if you think it's important.' The older ones nodded uncomfortably. Alice scowled.

CHAPTER FOURTEEN

William Montgomery, 70, 5'10", grey hair: I heard Debs giving them instructions before the search even started. I climbed down from the music tree and walked towards them.

The first girl I saw was Rosie, the eleven-year-old who'd seen me after the crash. When she saw me, she screamed. I spoke reassuringly to her, but she turned and bolted for the beach.

I followed her, more slowly, still talking. When I got into the open, I stood, unthreateningly, with my hands hanging loose by my sides. It was the first time in two weeks I'd stood on the beach in daylight. I lifted my face to the sun and felt almost at peace, better than I had for weeks. Whatever the minor irritations that the company of the girls would certainly provide, hiding from them had become ridiculous.

Debs emerged from the bushes, running. She let off the rape alarm and then they all started to come from the bushes. Rosie was still screaming in little bursts. I went on talking reassuringly.

'Shurrup,' Debs said. 'Shut your face. We know all about you.'

'What do you know?' I said calmly, intending to defuse her near-hysteria. She was obviously angry, apparently at me. The older girls looked awkward. Now Debs was there the younger ones clustered behind her, at a respectful distance from her, looking frightened.

Alice was neither awkward nor frightened. She seemed pleasantly surprised. She stood confidently, secure in her outstanding good looks, and smiled. She's a boring individual, but Lord she's beautiful.

'Hi. I'm Alice,' she said. 'And you are?'

'William Montgomery. How do you do?' I said.

'SHURRUP!' shouted Debs.

Alice smiled forgivingly. 'Chill out, Debs,' she said. 'Hey, c'mon guys, introduce yourselves.'

'I'm Emma,' said Emma, and the others followed suit.

Debs stood apart, irresolute, still obviously angry, but also on the point of tears. Now there was no one behind her, since the rest of the group was round me, she was uncertain.

'I read what you wrote bout us,' she said. 'I read it.'

I felt a spurt of anger, on my own account, and a reflex response to hers. I forced myself to say calmly, 'It wasn't intended for anyone's eyes but mine. I must apologise to you all for not coming forward earlier. I felt ill, after the crash.'

'Yeah,' said Alice. 'It was a trauma. We all felt traumatised. Really traumatic.'

'We gonna eat, or what?' said Rouchelle.

'Good idea,' said Emma. 'Lunch. Good idea.'

Debs opened her mouth, and shut it again.

'Yeah,' said Alice. 'Breadfruit. Great.'

Anneka, 11, 5'1", mousy hair: He was tall and very very old. But he was nice. He had a smiley face. I'd been scared before I saw him, cos of Debs being horrible. We were all scared I think. She'd just kind of exploded. PMS, could be. So we all went to search, she told us to. Susan was crying. Nobody said anything cos we were scared Debs'd shout at us. Emma too, I think, but she could of been just being tactful. Rohini wasn't with us, I looked, and I wanted her there.

But with the man there it was all right, suddenly. Debs kind of shrivelled, like an old balloon, and we all said hello to him and walked back down to the fire for lunch, and some of us chatted to him and he chatted back, and then when we were having lunch Rohini came and said she'd been for a walk up the mountain. Rohini seemed to know the man before.

I sat right by him and he talked to me lots. He's a granpa too, two of his grandchildren are girls, one just my age. He really likes them, he talked all about them, then he asked me all about me, and the same with the other kids, and it was all like better than normal, it was all happy. Like being rescued, acksherly, but not just from the island. Like being happy all through, happy now and happy for what's next, cos the rescuers would come and I'd go back to Granpa with a friend.

Rohini, 17, 5'2", black hair: Dr Montgomery's public property now. I only feel a little bit jealous. It had been foolish to think of him as mine, and to be disappointed by his reaction to me in the first place. I'm pleased to see that the others've accepted him so

209

readily. They seem relieved to have an adult about, and I certainly am.

I join the group sitting in the sand around Dr Montgomery and nibble at a banana to look as if I'm taking part in the general event. The ickles are behaving like eight-year-olds with a long-lost but theoretically much-loved uncle, showing off and giggling and doing handstands in the sand (I didn't know they could). The rest of us are like a group of prefects making polite conversation with a visiting lecturer, apart from Alice. She arranges herself on the sand beside him, one almost-bare leg stretched out, the other bent at the knee, her hands clasped round the bent knee. It is effective, but, I reflect cheerfully, must already be profoundly uncomfortable. With any luck she'll lock in that position permanently.

Emma, who'd started out quite far away from me, gradually shuffles herself round so she can talk, quietly.

'Where'd you go?' she says.

'Up to the skull shrine,' I say.

'Why didn't you tell me?'

'Why should I?' I say sharply, irritated by her posses-siveness. She doesn't respond to what I've said, or my tone.

'Debs went demented,' she whispers.

'What about?' I said.

'Partly about the man. She said I'd been lying to her. What did she mean?'

'No idea,' I say.

'Where did she get your rape alarm?'

'I think Tamsin must've nicked it. Or she did.' I'm annoyed about that, too.

Emma snaps, really angry. 'This is serious. Listen to me. We've got to talk.' Rouchelle and Tawheeda, the closest to us, look curious. 'Debs kept saying she knew about *terrible things*. What did she mean?'

'No idea,' I say, and smile reassuringly at the other heads that are beginning to turn towards us. 'Keep it quiet. Everything's ticking over fine.'

'No it isn't,' she says. 'Debs is up to something.'

'Why don't you ask her?'

'Can't. She's not here. Neither is Tamsin or Nadia. Debs was *vicious*, Rohini. *Listen* to me.'

'Don't worry about it,' I say. Rather nastily, actually. I am angrier than I'd thought, underneath. Dr Montgomery, who I want to talk to, doesn't particularly want to talk to me. Emma, who I don't specially want to talk to, wants me to report my intentions and thoughts hourly. And now she's doing a stupid female over-reaction. Debs has always been vicious except when she plays nice for her fantasy cameras. Probably she's just worked out there aren't any.

Nadia, 14, 5'6", redhead: I can hear them talking from here. The man's there. There was a man, and Rohini hadn't played a trick. I'd sort of guessed that.

I don't care. I don't care about anything. Yes I do, I care about everything. No I don't. I'll just sit up here in a sort of hide halfway between the caves and the clearing. I won't think.

When you say you won't think, you can't really stop it. The only way is to flood the bad thinks out with good thinks. I try. I try to think about what I'll draw next, but drawing — no, don't think.

Debs knows. *I* don't even know I know, but Debs knows. You're a dyke, Nadia, she said. You're a lesbo, you're a stinking dyke. It was the Alice drawings I'd made. Alice, Barbarian Queen. They were well done. I was pleased with them, except the foot on one of them wouldn't go right.

Tamsin'd stolen them, spiteful little cow, and I hadn't even noticed they'd gone. When Debs was talking at me – her voice all poisonous and . . . just poisonous, she's gone weird, like there's no one there behind her eyes except poison – when Debs was talking at me Tamsin was dancing round with the drawings in her hand kind of taunting me with them. She could do with a good slap, Tamsin.

Debs said when the rescuers came she'd tell them about me and then it would be all over the world everywhere, everyone would know. They'd know in Eltham and there aren't any gays in Eltham except for the ones we laugh at. Not that *I* know. Not *normal* people. I'm not gay. I just don't like boys yet. I'm not going to tell my mum. She's proud of me. When I won she said, Now everyone will know you've got a gift, Nadia, not just me and the art teacher. I want my mum to hug me. Would she hug me? Debs said there'd be a meeting and if I took her side she wouldn't tell everyone. Can't trust her. Didn't go to the meeting, missed the meeting. Maybe her side is the right side, then I'll take it. No, missed the meeting, don't have to take a side.

I'm not going down.

I want my mum.

Alice, 18, 5'8", mid-brown hair with red highlights: The doctor man really fancied me, I could tell. Now he's here he can take over, run things, I don't think he's too old to do that, and he's not done any of it so far and it's really hard work. For instance I've gotta walk all the way down to the baggage with Rohini to get some batteries n stuff. She does have some more, thought she did. All that walking just for tonight's party, just so the kids can have a good time.

William Montgomery, 70, 5'10", grey hair: The girls are very tiring. I escaped to have a rest, and I slept. On the beach, under the shade of the trees, north of the fire and their clearing. I don't think any of them have gone that far north. The sand is clear and white and warm, with none of their footmarks on it. Hiding, I've missed the beach.

They're all talking eagerly about the party and rehearsing their turns. Each of them has to provide an entertainment of some kind. My heart sinks at the prospect. I'll obviously have to attend, though.

I shall present it as a play. Depending on their choice of performance, it might even turn out to be a musical.

The Party on Saturday Evening

CAST: as for 'The Meeting on the Second Day, except for the loss of THE BABY and the addition of THE MAN.

Evening, before supper, around the fire. The fire flickers, becoming more visible all the time as twilight approaches. Around it, food is laid out on coconut shells: baked bread-fruit, sliced coconut flesh, heaps of bananas, and a rich red indigenous fruit somewhat resembling a plum. Shells full of water and coconut milk are balanced on rocks between the fire and the clearing. The silent CD player is ceremonially ensconced on a specially constructed plat-form of piled stones surmounted by a large flat stone of appropriate size.

THE MAN *is standing at a comfortable distance from the fire. He has changed into clean but crumpled trousers and shirt. His feet are bare.* ANNEKA *is beside him, chatting. As the girls arrive, singly and in groups, they go to greet him. The younger ones are bizarrely dressed in an assort-ment of their plunder, with painted faces, and they come from the clearing, chattering and giggling loudly. The older ones are dressed and made-up as for a party,* ALICE *and*

DEBS *with elaborate fake jewellery on their torsos.* THE MAN *compliments the girls on their appearance.*

EMMA *stands near the fire and claps her hands.*

EMMA: *(loudly)* OK, everyone, I think we're all here. Shall we start? Alice?

ALICE: Hi, guys, quiet up now, shush shush shush. What we're gonna do, we'll do our talent spot first, then we'll eat, then we'll dance for as long as the batteries last, OK? Is that Nadia back there? Hey, Nadia, where's your party clothes?

The others turn to look. NADIA, *still wearing the competition-issue shorts and shirt, grins and shakes her hair free.*

NADIA: My hair's ready to party.

MOST OF THE GIRLS: *(THE ICKLES particularly shrill and hysterical)* Yay . . . way to go . . . party party party.

DEBS *looks at her.* NADIA *looks away.*

ANNEKA: Where's Susan?

THE ICKLES: *(slightly discomfited, still erratically loud)* No idea . . . in the clearing . . . isn't she here . . . no idea . . . party party . . .

TAMSIN: *(boldly)* She's probly still on the rock.

ANNEKA: Which rock?

THE ICKLES: No rock . . . I never . . . no idea . . . what rock?

ANNEKA: *(agitated)* Not the top rock? *(To* THE MAN.*)* She can't see to get down from there . . . I never let her go there . . . Susan . . .

THE MAN: Shall we go and see?

SUSAN *(off)* screams. *Sound of a fall. Appalled silence.*

TAMSIN: She should of been supervised.

THE MAN *and* ANNEKA *exit, left.* ROHINI, ROUCHELLE *and* THE GOODY-GOODS *follow.*

NADIA: *(to Tamsin)* You should of been strangled at birth.

ALICE: *(concerned face)* That's not very nice, Nadia.

THE ICKLES: *(interspersed with sobs)* We told her not to . . . we said . . . we said not to . . . I never . . . she shouldn't of . . .

EMMA: Hush, everyone, let's just wait and see, hush . . .

They sob into silence and the whole group is silenced, listening. ANNEKA *(off) walls inconsolably.* VANESSA *re-enters. She is shocked and crying, but trying to keep her voice steady.*

VANESSA: I'm sorry, everyone, there's been a dreadful accident. SUSAN – she's slipped and fallen. I'm afraid she's . . . I'm afraid she's dead. DR MONTGOMERY says her neck is broken, there's nothing we can do.

EMMA: *(stricken)* Oh no, oh no, oh no . . . *(Pulls herself together.)* Right, everyone, no party of course, all stay here for the minute, just stay here . . .

EMMA *starts to leave for the clearing but is met by the others, returning.* THE MAN *is carrying* ANNEKA *in his arms, curled up against his chest.* ROHINI *is carrying an empty whisky bottle. She and* ROUCHELLE *are talking to each other, inaudibly.* THE GOODY-GOODS, *arms interlinked, are crying.* TAWHEEDA *is praying.*

ROUCHELLE: *(to* TAMSIN, *angrily)* You spiteful little cow. *(To* THE ICKLES, *sorrowfully.)* You should've known better.

TAMSIN: What right you got, blaming me? I'm a kid. I should of been looked after. You should of looked after me. All of us, we're kids. An it was down to Susan, her decision, she decided, her decision . . .

THE ICKLES: She decided . . . she said . . . she wanted to . . . I never . . .

ALICE: Hey, no blame, no blame, let's not do the blame thing.

ROHINI: *(to* TAMSIN, *showing her the empty bottle)* You stole the whisky and gave it to them. They're all drunk. Thief. Stupid, stupid, selfish little thief.

THE ICKLES: *(in real alarm and guilt)* Hardly any . . . I never . . . just a bit, to try . . . we're not drunk, when my sister's drunk she throws up an passes out . . .

ANNEKA: *(to* THE MAN, *who is now sitting on the sand beside her, exhausted)* Poor Susan, poor poor Susan. She was nearly happy. So was I. *(Serious question.)* Doesn't it ever work out? Is it always like that, you think it's all right and it isn't?

THE MAN: *(to* ANNEKA*)* No, not always. Not even often.

ANNEKA: You sure?

THE MAN: Quite, quite sure. Often, it works out.

ANNEKA: Not for Susan. Not this time. And she doesn't have another time.

DEBS: *(harshly, cutting through the universally muted atmosphere)* I'm gonna give you my talent. I'm gonna do my turn.

Universal murmurs of surprise and demurral.

EMMA: *(firmly)* No, Debs. Not now. We won't . . .

DEBS: *(vehemently)* Yes I WILL. My talent is sussing it, what's goin on. I know what's been goin on. I'm gonna tell you why it all happened. It isn't the ickles' fault, or Tamsin's. An I got evidence *(brandishes sheaves of paper)*.

TAMSIN: *(sullen)* Yeah, I said, not my fault.

THE ICKLES: *(mightily relieved)* Yeah . . . listen to Debs . . . Debs knows . . . I never . . .

EMMA: *(keeping exasperation under control)* Debs, this is *not* the time to give us your talent.

DEBS: *(viciously, to* EMMA*)* You lot, you lot, it's always the time for *your* talent, never the time for mine. Well this time it is, they want to hear, it wouldn't be fair not to listen, would it, Tamsin?

TAMSIN: Yeah, yeah, I want to hear. Gotta be fair. Gotta be heard.

THE ICKLES: *(shouting, still more relieved as the attention switches away from them)* Yeah . . . let's hear . . . gotta be fair . . . Debs . . . party party oops sorry . . .

DEBS: I gotta right to be heard, Alice, I gotta right. Say I gotta right. I'm grieving. I'm in shock. I gotta right.

ALICE: *(completely at sea mentally, physically composed and commanding)* I —

DEBS: Grief takes people different ways, this is my way, I gotta speak. For Susan.

ALICE: Yeah, that's right. Grief. Gotta speak for Susan. Go for it, Debs.

ROHINI: *(to THE MAN)* Stop this. You must stop this, now.

THE MAN: *(in extreme physical discomfort, pale, sweating. To ROHINI)* They're hysterical children. They're like a school of jellyfish. Nothing will stop them.

ROHINI: *(profoundly disappointed)* You mean you won't. Emma?

EMMA: *(loudly)* Please, everyone, let's be calm. Let's think a minute.

THE CAN'T BIRD: Caaan't, caaan't.

DEBS: *(shouting)* YES I CAN, YES I CAN, DON'T YOU TELL ME I CAN'T.

ALICE: *(mollifying)* OK, Debs, go ahead, speak for Susan.

DEBS: *(controlling herself, speaking evenly)* I spent a lot of time on this, worked it out, it's gotta be done the way I say. I talk. I ask questions, an the person I ask, they answer. No one else. OK, Alice?

ALICE: *(in a warmly understanding voice)* Sure, Debs, sure. Got that guys?

Murmur of agreement from the younger ones. EMMA *sits down. They all sit down except* ROHINI.

ROHINI: *(to* THE MAN*)* You've got to stop them.

THE MAN: *(stroking* ANNEKA's *hair gently, as she sobs)* It'll play itself out.

ROHINI: *(to* EMMA*)* Don't let them do this.

EMMA *opens her mouth to speak, but is overridden.*

DEBS: You heard the rules. You all heard the rules. I speak, you listen. Rohini wants to shut me up cos of what I know. I got evidence. You gotta listen, it's complicated, you gotta listen.

ALICE: *(supportively)* Yeah, we'll listen, won't we, guys?

DEBS: Right. First thing you gotta know, every morning Rohini digs up the bodies of the baby an its mother.

General astonishment and horror.

ROHINI: I —

DEBS: *(overriding)* You gotta SHURRUP, it's the rules, isn't it, Tamsin?

TAMSIN: Yeah. Yeah.

ROHINI: I —

DEBS: *(vicious)* IT'S THE RULES.

ROHINI *shrugs, withdrawing into herself, furious and disappointed.*

DEBS: Like I was saying, she digs up the bodies every morning, Tamsin's seen her. You seen her, didn't you?

TAMSIN: Yes, I seen her.

More astonishment and horror. They all look at ROHINI, who looks wearily out to sea.

DEBS: An now I'll tell you why. It's the island, the island we're on, it's alive, it's got spirits, evil spirits, like ghosts.

THE ICKLES: Yeah, Tamsin said . . . she said . . . like evil ghosts —

DEBS: Just listen. The island keeps its evil ghosts like mostly in one place, in an evil house with skulls, up at the top of the island, an Rohini saw it an she didn't say, she didn't say, cos she was like in a team with the evil ghosts, an she dug up the bodies cos the ghosts wanted bones an she did blood sacrifice, like in a vidjo I seen.

THE ICKLES: Yeah, I seen it too . . . I haven't, my mum doesn't prove of horror . . . was there a zombie 'swell . . . no that's another vidjo, with flesh dripping off . . . yuk, eeuch . . .

DEBS: Yeah, you know what I mean, you know what I mean.

TAWHEEDA: There's no such thing as ghosts, I –

DEBS: *(overriding)* Gotta keep to the rules, Tawheeda. Well, this island's, like, alive, and it's evil, and Rohini's sacrificing to it every morning, and the evil ghosts make bad things happen, like what happened to Susan. None of us done it, the island done it. And Rohini. That's the worst thing they done. But other evil things' swell.

TAMSIN: Tell us bout the other evil things.

THE ICKLES: Yeah, tell us . . . the island made us . . . I'd've been really nice to Susan normally, cos she couldn't see . . . yeah, me too . . . me too . . .

EMMA: This doesn't make sense. Rohini –

DEBS: *(overriding)* Gotta keep the rules. Respeck for Susan. We gorra give her respeck. Well, the island, this evil island we're on . . . (THE ICKLES *look at the sand they're sitting on and shift uncomfortably.*) . . . so the man came in, the island brought the man, an he watched us when we washed an when we weed an with no clothes on . . . (*Cries of embarrassment and shock.*) . . . an he wrote it down, I've got it here, he wrote it all down . . . an he killed the baby. (*Gasps of astonishment.*) Cos he's got, like, kids of his own, lots of kids, an he knew how to look after a baby, an he didn't. An I did my best, I did my best, an I couldn't . . .

ASSORTED VOICES, including EMMA: I know you did . . . Wasn't your fault, Debs . . . did your best . . .

THE MAN: If I could have helped, I would have.

DEBS: How many children you got?

THE MAN: Four, but –

DEBS: *(overriding)* An I spose you never did nothing, you never took care of the babies, you never did nothing.

THE MAN: No, but –

DEBS: *(cry of despair)* You should of. You should of. Men never help, but they should, they should.

Most of the group are staring at THE MAN.

AN ICKLE: My dad pissed off, just left us, for That Bitch.

ANOTHER ICKLE: An mine.

NADIA: *(matter-of-fact, impatient)* An mine, but that's nothing to do with this. All of this is crap.

DEBS: *(waving her sheaf of papers, pointedly, at* NADIA*)* Shurrup.

NADIA, *shocked, subsides.*

ALICE: My dads is great, he's great.

ANNEKA: And Granpa, Granpa's always . . .

DEBS: *(overriding, pointing at* THE MAN*)* An he wrote about us. He wrote about us, like we was beetles. Just like we was beetles. He said we was all the same an we was stupid. An he said I had dyed hair, just like . . . just like . . .

TAMSIN: You do have dyed hair.

DEBS: *(knowing she has a point, feeling deeply, but unable quite to articulate)* It's his fault. An all the men, it's their fault. We women do all the work, all the time, all the real work what no one pays you for like children an sick people an food an washing an cleaning an men do the work you get paid like real money for, like a game, in the meeja or in like banks, an it's play work, an the other work is work, an women do it an don't get paid, an then they just look at you like they've got a right an they say, an they say you're not good enough, you got dyed hair.

THE MAN: *(quietly)* I'm sorry, Debs.

DEBS: Sorry doesn't cut it. Like you couldn't tell us apart. Like we were all the same, just like age an height an hair, that's all we are to you, all we are, an we're more than that, an you just hide away in the trees an talk about yourself all the time an your feelings, an how you don't want us to talk to you, 'sif we wanna talk to you, cos you don't listen you just wanna look, and see us washing and weeing an on the website, an you lot've taken the ejucation too, like years an years an years you've had an I've had none, jus no time to sit in trees an listen to dead music and read dead books an use long words wot nobody needs, an I'M NOT STUPID! AN I'M MORE THAN HAIR! We're all more than hair, get it? Guys? We're more than hair?

TAMSIN: Yeah, sure. *(Chants.)* More than hair! More than hair!

THE ICKLES: *(enthusiastically)* More than hair! More than hair!

The older ones demur, protest quietly, talk among themselves. THE MAN *shakes his head wearily.* ANNEKA *clutches on to him, anxious.* ROHINI *walks away from the group, towards the sea. She is looking at something on the horizon.*

DEBS: *(waving her arms in a downward motion, quietening the chant)* Yeah, yeah, you're right, we're more than hair. An we seen through it now, the evil island an the ghosts an the bones, an Rohini's blood sacrifice like in the vido, an all the bad things like the baby and Susan, all the bad things, an not rescuing us, not looking out for us, not coming to get us and give us what we was PROMISED, PROMISED.

TAMSIN: *(chanting)* Prom-issed, prom-issed.

THE ICKLES: *(chanting)* Prom-issed, prom-issed, prom-issed.

DEBS: An leavin us here, no proper food, gettin burnt by the sun, gettin the runs, jus cos they wanted the pickshers, jus cos they wanted . . . just us to look at . . . just us to look at . . . *(Tails off, takes a deep breath.)* An so, what we've gorra think now, this evil island man what's bin looking at us, at the kids too, he's no more than a pedo. He *is* a pedo, a pedo.

THE ICKLES: *(screaming)* Pedo . . . pedo . . . pedo . . .

TAMSIN: Nail him to the trees by his bollocks, my mum says.

AN ICKLE: We got no nails.

TAMSIN: We got trees.

AN ICKLE: What's bollocks?

EMMA: *(standing up, loudly)* Stop this, Stop this, now. We're all upset. Calm down.

DEBS: 'Sall right for you, 'sall right for you, you've got it made, posh bitch, posh bitch, posh tall blonde bitch, I'm gonna show you what we do, we gonna show him, pedo, he can't do this to us, we was promised, watch what we do.

They all watch her, mesmerised by her passionate force. She raises her arms, letting the papers flutter away from her hands. Caught by the breeze, the papers float and eddy round her. Some drift into the fire and flame up. Slowly, she starts to move in Nadia's bug dance.

DEBS: *(chanting)* Another man bites the sand, squish. Another man bites the sand, squash.

NADIA: Hey –

DEBS: *(briefly still, overriding)* SHURRUP.

EMMA: STOP IT! NOW!

DEBS: *(moving with energy and purpose)* Another man bites the sand, squish! Another man bites the sand, squash! C'mon! We gorra show him! Pedo! Pedo!

226

TAMSIN *and* THE ICKLES *scramble up with cries of* 'Pedo! Pedo!' *and join her. The dance is beginning to take shape, and the chant gaining power. They are still some yards away from* THE MAN, *who is watching them quizzically with no sign of moving.*

ROHINI: *(from her position on the shore)* Hey, Alice –

ALICE: *(interested)* What?

DEBS: *(shouting, drowning* ROHINI *out)* We gorra SHOW HIM! C'MON!

The dancing group, chanting more loudly and stamping more emphatically, approach THE MAN. *He starts to get up.* DEBS *darts forward and shoves him over.* ANNEKA *tries to cover his body with hers.*

GROUP: ANOTHER MAN BITES THE SAND, SQUISH! ANOTHER MAN BITES THE SAND, SQUASH!

They stamp on whatever part of THE MAN *they can locate, and sometimes on* ANNEKA. EMMA, NADIA, ROUCHELLE *and* TAWHEEDA *try to intervene.* VANESSA *and* MEI LIN, *standing by, terrified, try to hold* CHARLOTTE *back, but she pulls away from them angrily and joins the older ones in pulling* THE ICKLES *away.*

ROHINI: *(calmly but very loudly)* Rescuers! Rescuers! Alice! A camera crew!

ALICE: *(commandingly, adjusting her expression and her body jewellery)* Knock it off, you guys! Stop it! We're being rescued!

The approaching craft, a launch, is now quite close, inside the lagoon. On the prow, A MAN with a camera, filming. TAMSIN and THE ICKLES step back. DEBS is still stamping, but with less purpose. She gradually stops. EMMA checks ANNEKA, who is bruised and quietly crying, but otherwise all right. EMMA checks THE MAN. He is not breathing. She begins CPR. ROHINI joins her, and helps. The camera is now filming their efforts. ALICE joins EMMA and ROHINI, and gets in the way. TAWHEEDA is praying. NADIA is watching. All the others look at the camera.

PR MAN: *(from the boat)* Doctor! Doctor!

KEN WRIGHT: *(from the boat)* Medical assistance there! Now!

A beautiful female doctor, CAROLYNN, 29, 5'7", blonde, leaps out of the boat carrying a bag and sprints splashing through the shallows. She briefly consults with EMMA and ROHINI, then takes over care of THE MAN.

The boat has grounded in the shallows. Its occupants splash to shore, with the exception of KEN WRIGHT, who directs operations from the boat. Three cameras are now filming, one directed at the resuscitation attempt, one on ALICE, and one a wide shot including EMMA. There is general confusion and several unrelated conversations.

ANNEKA: *(to EMMA and ROHINI)* Is he OK? Is he OK?

ROHINI: *(gently)* Maybe not. He's very ill, Anneka, his heart . . . He could've died at any time. Any strain . . .

228

ANNEKA: But he *carried* me . . . he carried *me* . . . it might've killed him, an he *carried* me.

EMMA: You're skinny, you're light. That'd've been fine. It was the stamping, it was the stamping that did it, oh I should've stopped them, I should've stopped them.

ANNEKA: *(loyally)* You tried, you tried really hard, you tried . . . oh Susan . . . oh poor Susan . . .

ROHINI: *(to* EMMA*)* Not your fault. To you, they were just kids, bullying. I should have stopped them. *I* knew.

EMMA: Knew what?

ROHINI: About his heart

EMMA: How?

ROHINI: He told me

EMMA: *(shocked)* You *talked* to him? And you didn't tell me?

ROHINI: *(sincerely)* Sorry.

EMMA: *(equally sincerely)* That's OK.

ANNEKA: Emma, what'd he say? He said something, he was looking at Alice when you shouted at her about the cameras, Rohini, he looked at her and he said something. I couldn't hear it.

EMMA: Something about *Ready for the closeup now, mister*, something . . . oh!

She looks at ROHINI. *They speak together.*

EMMA and ROHINI: Ready for the closeup now, Mr de Mille.

ROHINI: I don't think we've got it quite right.

EMMA: Who cares?

ANNEKA: But what's that *mean*?

ROHINI: It means he's very brave, and he was quoting and making a joke, and he thinks Alice is silly.

ANNEKA: Alice *is* silly.

THE DOCTOR, *shaking her head, covers* THE MAN's *face and says something to the adults round her.* ANNEKA *sobs.* TAWHEEDA, *head bent, is praying. The boat's* CREW *have hurriedly put together a construction of flat stones topped by a tarpaulin, and* KEN WRIGHT *walks to shore dry-footed.*

DEBS: *(a little distance away, to one of the* BOAT PARTY*)* You a journalist?

PR MAN: No, I'm in public relations.

DEBS: Like, putting the best on things, putting a spin?

PR MAN: *(smiling widely)* Sometimes, yes. We're all very, very happy that you're safe, we'll get you home soon —

DEBS: *(overriding)* Cos I gotta story here, I gotta story, know any tabloids?

PR MAN: *(smiling less widely)* Mr Wright owns three. But as for your story, part of the rules of the competition —

DEBS: *(overriding)* Sod your rules, his crap plane nearly killed us, we could of died, I gotta story the *other* tabloids, the tabloids he *doesn't* own, they'd give me money for this story.

PR MAN: *(not smiling at all)* Of course we could take another look at the rules . . .

Meanwhile, ROHINI *approaches a sobbing* NADIA. *After a brief conversation between them,* NADIA *sits down and sketches rapidly while* ROHINI *gathers the scattered papers, checks through them and bums some.* ROHINI *then takes two sketches from* NADIA, *adds them to her paper pile, and brings them to the* PR MAN.

ROHINI: Nadia's such a great artist, look at all these drawings she's done, all of the parrots and the bats and the plants. Aren't they great? Isn't it weird, she's never drawn us while we were here −

DEBS: *(overriding)* Oh yes, she's drawn *one* −

ROHINI: *(overriding)* Just what I was going to say. She's drawn one of us and I'm very honoured that it's me.

ROHINI: *shows the* PR MAN *a hurried but skilful and flattering sketch of a reclining* ROHINI, *de-emphasising her moustache. The* PR MAN *is apparently delighted.*

DEBS: *(to* NADIA*)* See if I care. I'm gonna be laughing anyway, you'll see.

The BOAT PARTY *are now giving orders, marshalling the* SURVIVORS *into position for a set-piece speech from* KEN WRIGHT. *The* CAMERAMEN *take their places and a* SOUND RECORDIST *and his* ASSISTANT *fuss with equipment.* KEN WRIGHT *stands near the fire,* THE GIRLS *around him,* ALICE *one side,* EMMA *the other.* THE ICKLES *are fetchingly and leggily positioned in front.*

PR MAN: Looking good. Looking good, tall girl in a bit. *(To* TAWHEEDA.*)* That's it, next to the blonde one. *(To* ROHINI.*)* Bit further over, my love, looking good, OK for cameras.

CAMERAMEN: OK . . . goddit . . . OK.

PR MAN: OK for sound?

SOUND MAN: OK for sound.

PR MAN: Mr Wright?

KEN WRIGHT: I —

TAMSIN: *(loudly)* You should of come sooner.

DEBS: *(viciously)* Shurrup, stupid little cunt.

KEN WRIGHT: *(to the* PR MAN*)* We won't use that.